DATE DUE

THE BOOK OF
BAD THINGS

The Book of
Bad Things

Dan Poblocki

SCHOLASTIC PRESS · NEW YORK

All rights reserved. Published by Scholastic
Press, an imprint of Scholastic Inc., *Publishers
since 1920*. SCHOLASTIC, SCHOLASTIC PRESS,
and associated logos are trademarks and/or
registered trademarks of Scholastic Inc.

No part of this publication may be reproduced,
stored in a retrieval system, or transmitted
in any form or by any means, electronic,
mechanical, photocopying, recording, or
otherwise, without written permission of
the publisher. For information regarding
permission, write to Scholastic Inc., Attention:
Permissions Department, 557 Broadway, New
York, NY 10012.

Library of Congress Cataloging-in-Publication
Data Available

ISBN 978-0-545-64553-9

10 9 8 7 6 5 4 3 2 1   14 15 16 17 18

Printed in the U.S.A.   23

First edition, September 2014

The text type was set in Adobe Caslon.
Book design by Christopher Stengel

For Amanda

URSULA & THE HOUSE

WHERE IS IT?

Ursula pawed carefully through the looming stacks of cardboard boxes.

Where did it go?

Her mind raced, but she forced herself to move slowly, as if that might quiet the voice screaming in her head. Inside every carton, she discovered only disappointment and dust and the useless junk she'd been unable to toss out for years. A painful pressure was building behind her eyes. It felt as though her ears were stuffed with marshmallows.

I'm sure I saw it only a few months ago!

The old woman clamped her lips upon a small box of matches. If she didn't locate the lighter fluid now, tonight, she knew she may never have another chance. Something was wrong deep inside her chest. A painful rattle. For the past few days, she'd struggled for breath, wheezing, as if her lungs had shrunk to the size of raisins. Ursula was no fool. She hadn't been to a doctor in maybe a decade, but she knew what was growing inside of her.

Darkness was coming. It was a shadow she'd felt wavering at the edges of her vision for years.

But it wasn't her own death that frightened her.

Ursula stood in her living room, or what had once been a living room, and blinked away tears. Every inch of the place was a mess: bundles of newspapers and magazines and junk mail, bags of garbage and soiled clothes, and dried things that had once been food. From the floor to the ceiling, she'd stacked boxes she'd labeled with black marker again and again as the clutter had accumulated and changed and had tried to change her too. Ursula had fought it for as long she could, but by the time she'd discerned the depth of her predicament, she understood that there was no solution but the most drastic thing.

Her plan.

The first step was to remain calm. Stay quiet. Don't speak. Don't even think.

Where did I leave it?!

The first step was more difficult than she'd thought it would be.

The floor trembled. It knew. It heard her. A sudden pain split her forehead. Shadowy tendrils reached out to her, searching for a way into her skull. She was running out of time.

Hurry, you old fool!

The second step was to wet the room with the flammable liquid. Slowly. Gently. As if watering a garden. An everyday occurrence. A chore.

The house lurched, and the stacked boxes teetered toward her. She raised her arms to steady the closest ones, but something was mashing the inside of her chest, and she crumpled to her knees. The matchbox slipped from her mouth and matches spilled onto the floor.

Cartons tumbled, the weight of them smashing into Ursula's back. She fell over. Gasping for breath, she slapped the piles of junk away from her.

The ceiling was blurry. She was too weak now to stand, but she glanced around, hoping that by some miracle the tin had fallen nearby. No such luck. The lighter fluid was still hiding. The limited light that filtered through the shaded windows during the day disappeared with the setting of the sun, and evening shadows lapped at her like waves.

She pursed her lips and set her brow.

Forget step two. She still had step three and a seed of hope. Strike a match. Burn it all.

If tonight was the night that life was to abandon her, Ursula had to know that none of her possessions, the things she'd collected for years, would leave this house. It all must burn with her. She thought of that old saying, the one about how all of our worldly belongings remain behind when we die: *You can't take it with you.* If her plan succeeded, no one else would take it either.

The matchbox lay several inches from her face. A single match was beside it. With shaking hands, she took up the box and then clawed at the match, and for a moment, she remembered playing pick-up sticks with her brother and sister across an ocean. Unsteadily, she held the stick to the flint, suddenly overcome with the weight of what she was doing. This house had been her life. The things that surrounded her, *The Collection*, had become her reason for living. But she'd never imagined it would end her life. She cursed her uncle Aidan for leading her here, for leaving her this house, this burden.

She struck the match. A spark. A flame. In her surprise that it had worked, that the air had allowed the fire to bloom, the breath she'd been seeking all night long slipped from her lips and huffed out the light.

The floor trembled. The walls creaked. She knew that the *something* was laughing at her, but she had no voice to shout back. To tell it to shut up. And even if she had, her mind had begun to erase the words she might have used.

The shadows danced closer along the edges of her vision. She stared at the ceiling as it shrunk, smaller and smaller, into a dusty oval shape, an echo of the old woman's blue lips, silent, still, unable to take in even one last gasp before the mantle of darkness engulfed her entirely.

Cassidy's Book of Bad Things, Entry #52:
PARASITES

Parasites are creatures that keep themselves alive by invading or infecting the body of another living thing. This other living thing is called the host. The parasite feeds off the host, drinking its blood or eating it from the inside. Sometimes, the host dies. Then the parasite or the parasite's little parasite babies move on to find another host to torture and kill.

Although plenty of parasites are bad, I think one of the most horrible parasites is the tongue-eating louse. Even the name is enough to make you want to gag.

Every kid has heard of lice, at least at <u>my</u> school. A single lice is called a louse. They're the tiny bugs that sometimes live in your hair. My friend Janet caught them when she was really little. She says they bite and they're itchy, but you can wash them away with a special shampoo, so it isn't a big deal.

But there is a kind of louse that lives in the ocean that can grow quite large and disgusting. It swims inside the mouth of a fish and attaches itself to the fish's tongue. Then, it slowly eats the tongue until there's nothing left but a little stub inside the fish's mouth. And worse, after that, it latches onto the stub and stays there, <u>permanently</u>, pretending to be the fish's <u>new</u> tongue. And it survives by living off whatever the fish eats, nibbling any food that passes by on the way to the fish's stomach. And there's nothing the fish can do about it.

I am glad that I am not a fish. OR a louse!!!

CHAPTER ONE

CASSIDY BEAN CLOSED her notebook and glanced out the bus window. The world outside was a blur of green. She blinked several times, trying to capture mental snapshots of the scenery. A field of young corn. A tilted barn. Unending hills, lush with summer growth.

Having traveled nearly an hour from New York City already, Cassidy knew she was close to Whitechapel. The landscape was a good gauge. Fifteen minutes out: the yellow grasses of the Meadowlands and the yellow air above Elizabeth, New Jersey. Twenty minutes out: the broken sidewalks and graffiti-covered concrete walls of Newark's side streets. Thirty minutes out: the ramshackle Victorian houses of Maplewood, Milburn, and Summit, surrounded by the first real vision of green and leaves and flowers and trees. Forty: the suburban sprawl of the towns and the malls just off Route 78. Fifty: the ridge and the sky and the purple distance of a western eternity . . . and beyond.

Here, at an hour out, the bus had begun its lazy descent toward the Delaware River, where another of New Jersey's great ridges met the state of Pennsylvania.

Cassidy wouldn't get that far. The hamlet where the Tremonts lived was nestled in a warrenlike grouping of peaks and valleys a couple miles north of the highway. Soon, the bus would stop at a small shopping center a few miles before the first visible twist of the upcoming river. That parking lot was where Mrs. Tremont had promised she'd be waiting with Joey to bring her the rest of the way to their home, a house where Cassidy had spent the past two summers as part of a program that brought city kids out to the countryside.

This summer was to be her third with the Tremonts. It was also to be her last. Next year, Cassidy would turn thirteen. Too old for the program. And so this was it: *Whitechapel — The Final Chapter.*

She drummed her fingers nervously on the cover of the notebook in her lap — a cheap journal with a black-and-white marbled cardboard cover that her next-door neighbor had given to her a few years back. The Tremonts had not finalized their decision to accommodate Cassidy until the previous week. The past couple of months had delivered a nerve-wracking series of *almost-nots* and *wait-and-sees*. What hurt was feeling that the Tremonts didn't want her back again. But now she knew that wasn't true. They'd said yes. Finally. Yes.

Dennis and Rose were like the dad and mom she'd always dreamed of. They treated her like one of their own children. One night, a couple years ago, after Rose had scolded her for leaving a bowl of melted ice cream on the coffee table in the living room, Cassidy had gone to sleep wearing a smile, pleased that Rose had spoken to her the same way she'd speak to Tony or Deb or Joey.

Tony, the oldest of the Tremonts' three, was in college in Virginia where he spent summers working internships. Cassidy stayed in his bedroom, and whenever he'd visited while she was there, he'd slept on the pull-out couch in the den. Deb was in high school and spent most of her time with her older friends. But Cassidy and Joey were the same age, ten that first summer, and had become fast friends. They'd ridden bikes to the town pool, hiked the trails through the nearby state parks, trekked to the Dairy Queen for Blizzards, plopped exhausted onto the patio furniture out back, swatting at mosquitos, telling each other ghost stories late into the night.

The house in Whitechapel felt more like home than the apartment she shared with her mom, in the supposed *center-of-everything*, ever could.

When her social worker had called and told her that "the placement" had gone through, she'd run upstairs to tell Janet and Benji, her best friends in the apartment building. They were disappointed she was leaving them, but she promised to send postcards and they pretended to cheer up. That night, her mother had been as unexcited as she'd been the first two summers, but Cassidy was used to her mother's eye rolls, her tight lips, her silences. Later, wrapped up in the afghan quilt on the couch in the small living room, Cassidy couldn't sleep. The social worker's words ran through her head, two in particular: *host family*. Something about the term had bothered Cassidy, and it had continued to bother her for the next few days. The words echoed even as she climbed onto the bus at the Port Authority that morning.

Now, she drummed her fingers on the notebook cover again and shivered. The air-conditioning that had felt so nice an hour ago was suddenly overwhelming. She pulled a sweatshirt from the backpack on the seat beside her and slipped it over her shoulders, the sleeves extending over her chest like a pair of extra arms. She pressed her lips together and glanced down at the notebook — her journal, her *Book of Bad Things*. Five minutes ago, it came to her, the meaning of the words *host family*. She'd yanked the book from her bag, flipping through pages, desperate to find the relevant entry. It had been number fifty-two. Parasites. Parasites need *hosts* to live.

Cassidy squeezed her eyes shut. *Why did the Tremonts wait so long to say yes?* she wondered. *Why didn't they write to me this past year? Did I do something wrong?*

Yes, the previous summer had ended badly, but what had happened with Joey's dog, Lucky . . . That hadn't been her fault. Had it?

The driver eased toward the highway exit. They were almost there. Cassidy breathed deeply, counted to ten. She wanted this summer to be perfect. She wished to write lovely poems about it, maybe in a new journal for happy memories instead of in the book on her lap, the one she clung to like a weapon.

When the bus halted in front of the supermarket, she stood up, grabbed her backpack, and raced up the aisle. Outside, she glanced around quickly, but didn't see Rose's white hatchback. The driver handed over her bulky luggage, which she promptly dropped onto the pavement. She heard a crunching sound and her stomach squelched. There went the gifts she'd packed.

She dragged her belongings to the curb and watched as the driver sealed up the luggage compartment, climbed aboard, and shut the door. The bus shifted into reverse. She was thinking, as the bus pulled back like a curtain at a magic show, that Joey would be standing on the other side, waving excitedly at her, his mom beside him, a watchful hand on his shoulder. But when the bus moved out of its parking space and chugged forward, back toward the highway, Cassidy realized that she was alone.

The Tremonts hadn't shown up.

CHAPTER TWO

THE NOONDAY SUN glared from above, baking the sidewalk underneath her. The longer Cassidy sat, the damper she became. She barely had two inches of sleeve at her shoulder upon which to wipe her brow, and that had already been soaked through several times. She imagined that she looked like a drowned ferret — a great way to greet Joey after a year. She tucked the sweatshirt into her backpack.

After another twenty minutes, however, Cassidy understood that her damp hair, shiny skin, and itchy red eyes should be the least of her worries. Every vehicle that approached from the street made her sit up straight, but the hazy glare off the asphalt was blinding, and Cassidy could only gauge that they weren't coming for her when they continued on down the road. *They're just running late,* she told herself.

Unless the social worker had gotten it wrong.

The host family has decided to cleanse themselves of the parasite.

Cassidy shuddered and then stood, trying to think about what she and Joey would be doing later that day. A swim perhaps? Ice cream? A game of H-O-R-S-E in his driveway? What kinds of stories would he have to share? She wracked her mind for every interesting thing that had happened to her since she'd last been to Whitechapel, trying to cement the thoughts in place so there would be no awkward pauses in their conversation when he arrived.

After a while, she noticed that the sun had moved significantly across the sky. It had been more than an hour since the bus had gone. Maybe it was time to call someone. But what if, when she reached out to the Tremonts, they hung up on her, told her off . . . laughed?

Cassidy sat, removing her notebook and pen from her bag again. Turning to a fresh page, she swallowed down what felt like a large pebble creeping up her esophagus and then scribbled: *Entry #117 — Abandonment . . . Too many examples to note and not enough pages left.*

She scanned her words several times, felt her heartbeat slowing slightly and then smacked her tongue against her upper palate as moisture returned to her mouth. A momentary relief.

She knew that most of the kids who lived out here had cell phones and smart phones and the latest portable communication devices, but Cassidy had never owned one of her own. The city still had quite a few pay phones available if she needed to reach her mother. But the country is not the city. Glancing around the lot, she saw no phones.

Gathering herself together, she dragged her bags across the blistering sidewalk to the supermarket. The sensor flashed and the glass door slid open with a whoosh. Cold air blasted Cassidy's warm face. The store was almost entirely empty. A Beatles song played softly from hidden speakers. Of the twelve check-out lanes, only one was open, manned by a tall, thin teenage boy dressed in a black T-shirt, black jeans, and a red-vest uniform that sat wide on his bony shoulders. The boy was flipping through a comic book. He barely glanced up as Cassidy approached.

"Uh-um," Cassidy's voice broke. "Excuse me?"

The boy set the comic on the check-out belt and then brushed his long black bangs away from his forehead. His expression remained blank, as if he were staring at an empty space instead of a twelve-year-old girl.

"Can you help me?" she asked.

"Depends," said the boy.

Cassidy blushed. "On what?"

"On what kind of help you need." The boy blinked. "If you're being chased by a serial killer, I'd really rather just stay out of it. Collateral damage, you know?"

"I'm not . . . being chased. By anyone." She had no idea what he meant by *collateral damage*.

"Good. Then I'm pretty sure I can help you." He finally smiled. The flash of straight white teeth made him look mischievous.

"I just need to make a phone call."

The boy shrugged. "Easy enough," he said, pulling a cell out of his back pocket. Flipping it open, he asked, "What's the number?"

Shoot, Cassidy thought. *The number.* She dropped her bags and rifled through them. "I've got it somewhere . . . I hope. It's just that Mrs. Tremont was supposed to be here, like, I don't even know how long ago. I wanted to make sure I didn't make a mistake."

"I know the Tremonts," said the boy. "They live around the corner from me. I used to watch their son when he was little. In fact, I've got their number right here." The boy pressed a couple buttons and then handed the phone over.

Cassidy blinked, surprised. His face looked suddenly familiar. This was the boy who'd stayed with her and Joey once that first summer, when Dennis and Rose had concert tickets in the city. "Thanks," she whispered. Holding the receiver to her ear, she could hear the ringing.

There was a click and then a female voice answered, sounding annoyed. "What is it, Hal? I'm sort of busy here today."

"Mrs. Tremont?" Cassidy said. This was followed by a long moment of silence. "Are you there?"

"Cassidy! Oh my . . . You're at the Stop & Shop! I saw Hal's name and . . . What day . . . ?" The woman mumbled something.

"I'm *so* sorry, honey. Oh my goodness, you sit tight. I'll be *right* there."

Another click, followed by silence.

Cassidy handed the phone back to the boy behind the register. "All set?" he asked, looking pleased with himself.

"I hope so," she answered, her chest trembling. Mrs. Tremont had *forgotten* her? "Thanks . . . Hal."

"You're welcome, Cassie." When her mouth dropped open, Hal smirked even wider.

"You remember me?" She hated when people called her Cassie, but she was so surprised he'd come close that she didn't bother correcting him.

"Now I do. Same black hair. Same dimples. Same sparkly eyes. It's been a couple, but you don't look *that* different."

"You sure do."

He nodded. "Uh-huh. There are these things called growth spurts? Ever heard of them?"

Cassidy blushed. "Yes. I've heard of them."

"So you're back in Whitechapel for another few weeks?"

"My last summer. Next year I'll be too old."

"Too old? You? I don't believe it." Everything that came out of his mouth sounded like a joke.

"It's true. I'll be thirteen." When he didn't respond, she felt her cheeks growing warm again. "Mrs. Tremont is running late."

Hal shrugged. "Doesn't surprise me. It's been a big day over in Chase Estates."

A big day? "What do you mean?"

"Of course you haven't heard," he said, almost to himself. He sighed and then stared hard at her, as if formulating how to tell the story. "That crazy hermit lady who lived in the old farmhouse on the hill died." Cassidy shivered, raising her hands to her mouth. "There'd been this smell. . . . A couple days ago, when the police finally went in, they found her on the living room floor. She'd been there for a few days, ripening in the heat, surrounded by piles of junk. Stacks of it. Like, to the ceiling. People are saying she was a hoarder." Cassidy shook her head, confused. "A hoarder? You know, someone who can't throw anything away? It's some sort of mental disorder. OCD, I think. There was a whole television series about it. Anyway, my friends have been texting me all day. I guess the town's started clearing the garbage out of the house. Supposedly, they set up a few huge Dumpsters in her front yard, already filled with all sorts of stuff. I'm gonna paw through it when I get out of here. See if she had anything good."

Cassidy blinked back tears, trying to catch up. "Mrs. Chambers died?"

"Yeah! That was her name."

Now it all made sense. After what happened at the end of last summer, of course the Tremonts had forgotten about her today.

CHAPTER THREE

SEVERAL LONG MINUTES LATER, a car horn sounded from the parking lot. Hal had been telling her about his first year at college when Cassidy turned and saw the white hatchback idling at the curb.

"Gotta go! Thanks for letting me use the phone!"

"Anytime," said Hal. "Hey, I'll probably see you later on. Gonna head up to the Chambers place myself. Check things out."

The doors slid open, and the day's hot air pushed at Cassidy's chest like a pair of wide, angry hands.

The driver's-side door swung open and a tall, gangly woman leapt out. Mrs. Tremont. Rose. A kindergarten teacher during school months. A full-time mom during the summer. She maneuvered awkwardly around the door and then dashed in front of the car, her arms outstretched as if Cassidy were falling and she would catch her. Seconds later, Cassidy was enveloped in her host mother's arms, a pair of sinewy rubber bands squeezing away her breath. Cassidy smelled sweat on Rose's neck, masked by a baby powder scent. But mostly she smelled sweat. It wasn't unpleasant, just sudden and kind of weird.

"I'm so sorry," said Rose. She held Cassidy away, examining her from top to bottom. "Wow, you've gotten so tall!"

"There are these things called growth spurts," said Cassidy, forcing a grin.

Rose. Dark, thoughtful eyes. Brown hair trimmed short like a boy. There'd always been something about her that reminded Cassidy of a turtle, though she couldn't say what it was exactly. Her husky voice? Her serene demeanor? Her long neck?

"There certainly are," said Rose with a chuckle. "After raising three children into adolescence and beyond, I am familiar with growth spurts. Wait till you see Joey. Here, let me help you with your bags."

Cassidy handed over the suitcase and then followed Rose across the pavement. The sun was glaring off the car's windows, so she couldn't see inside. "What's wrong, he's too busy to step out and say hello?"

"Oh . . . well, he wasn't feeling well," said Rose. "But you'll see him soon enough at home."

Cassidy tried to respond, but all that came out of her mouth was a high-pitched grunt. Rose flung open the hatch in the rear of the car and placed the suitcase inside. Cassidy took a deep breath, carrying her backpack to the front seat. All those fears that had been swirling in her mind during the bus ride from the city bubbled up again.

Something strange was happening, not the least of which was the death of the Tremonts' neighbor, Ursula Chambers. Maybe that was all it was; the discovery of a dead body must have had some sort of weird effect on everyone who lived nearby. Hal, the grocery boy, had seemed downright giddy about it.

As soon as they'd buckled their safety belts and Rose had pulled away from the curb, Cassidy spoke up. Words to fill the silence. "Hal said Mrs. Chambers died."

Rose sighed. "Hal Nance has a big mouth."

"But it's true?" Cassidy ventured.

"Yes, it's true. In fact, that's the reason I was late." *The reason you forgot*, thought Cassidy. "Our street has been a complete mess. You'll see when we get there."

"Is it the reason Joey's not feeling well?"

Rose glanced at her, disconcerted. After a moment, she answered, "You'll have to ask him that yourself."

CHAPTER FOUR

NORTH OF THE SMALL SHOPPING CENTER, the land crested at a ridge blanketed with old-growth trees and marked with large, refurbished houses with frames dating back to before the American Revolution. On the other side of this hill, the road twisted and turned, following the natural gullies that steep streams and brooks had carved into the rocky ground, until it intersected Chapel Street, under which the waters joined, forming a churning river that roared westward. At this intersection of both streets and streams was Whitechapel proper, where a quaint collection of gift shops, general stores, and art galleries surrounded a magnificently maintained, white neo-Gothic church with a spire that strained toward heaven. The building had once been an Episcopalian place of worship, but like many things in the old town, it had long ago been renovated and repurposed — in this instance, for use as the town hall.

As Rose sped past the building, Cassidy bent her head to peer up at the steeple. She loved riding bikes with Joey down here. They'd perch on the wall by the bridge over the river, licking ice cream cones from the DQ, sitting in silence because the crashing sound of the congregating waters was too great to be heard over. She hoped they'd have the chance to do that again this summer.

The hatchback groaned as it made its way up into the steep countryside beyond the other side of the town. A few minutes past the next set of hills, the land opened up. Wide fields appeared before larger hills grew in the far distance.

Here were Whitechapel's farmlands, and though plenty of stock and produce was still traded from the area — New Jersey's famous fresh tomatoes, for example — the temptation of land development had proven too great for many of the farmers who'd been struggling for years to stay afloat. All along the next few miles of road, one subdivision sprawled after another. At the entry of each, a freshly painted sign demarcated which community was which: Summit Ranches, Headley Farms, and of course, Chase Estates, where the Tremonts resided.

Glancing ahead through the valley, Cassidy saw that these developments were still expanding. New houses sat next to newer mansions, each more grand than the last. As Rose pulled into her own development, Cassidy wondered when the construction would stop. What she had always cherished about her time here was the quiet, the sense of solitude, the air that you didn't have to share with millions of other people packed into tight apartment buildings while outside the sounds of cars honked at one another through unending flashing traffic signals. How much longer would it be before Whitechapel was just a more remote version of New York City? The thought of it made Cassidy feel empty, as though this were actually the last summer this place would exist. *As it is now,* she thought. *As I am now.*

Rose navigated up the labyrinthine streets of the Estates, and Cassidy's heart jangled like a squirrel in a cage. She'd barely spoken to Rose on the way here, and now she was closer than ever to seeing Joey again. He had always come along to pick her up. Why not this time? *You'll have to ask him that yourself,* Rose had said mysteriously.

Cassidy clutched the sides of the car seat as Rose pulled into the cul-de-sac, and finally, the steep driveway. At the top, the Tremont house was the same two-story, large gray box that she'd fallen in love with two years ago. The wide, white trimmed porch stretched across the front of the house, where Rose had arranged a collection of white wicker chairs and benches, iron plant stands overflowing with ferns and glossy green elephant ears four times the size of Cassidy's face. It was the perfect place to sit in the morning, sipping warm tea, watching as the sky turned from pink to a hazy summer blue.

Rose mentioned she had forgotten to pick up barbecue supplies for later, but she helped Cassidy bring her bags to the front door before making her way back to the hatchback and speeding off.

Cassidy felt a disturbing numbness when she realized she was alone. Well, not quite alone. About a dozen people had gathered up the street, gawking in front of the entrance to Ursula Chambers's long driveway. Deep in the woods, an impression of the dark old farmhouse was vaguely visible. Workers dragged what looked like bags and bags of garbage away from the building and down the path, tossing them into a Dumpster that was parked halfway up the driveway. Weeds and tall grass and even a few saplings had grown up through the gravel lane, threatening to block the way.

Memories of the previous summer raced through her mind: her suggestion to Joey that they try to make contact with Mrs. Chambers, the hike through the woods to the farmhouse's backyard, the confrontation, and then, of course, what happened later that night. . . . Cassidy blinked it all away and then shuddered, appalled at the way the neighbors were now behaving. Shouting. Pointing. Laughing. Cassidy took a deep breath, turned, and then reached out and opened the Tremonts' front door.

Chapter Five

"Hello?" she called out. "Anyone home?" She received no answer. The subtle scent of apples and cinnamon crept from the kitchen. The sound of muted music vibrated the floor above her head. Joey's room. Cassidy hiked her bag up on her shoulder, squeezed the suitcase's handle and then cautiously made her way up.

Joey's door was the first on the left. Cassidy knocked. The music inside seemed to grow louder. She knocked again, this time trying the knob. It wouldn't budge. Locked. Leaning forward, she pressed her lips to the crack at the edge of the door. She was about to call out so Joey could hear her over the stereo, when the door swung open. Joey gripped the knob fiercely, squinting into the darkness of the hallway. Cassidy was so surprised that she shouted his name anyway. At the same time he called out, "What do you want?" After a moment, Joey shook his head, clearing cobwebs. "Cassidy," he said. "Sorry. I thought you were my mom."

Not knowing how else to respond, she shrugged. "Rose dropped me off and went back out." When he rolled his eyes, she decided not to question why on earth he'd speak to his mother the way he'd just spoken to her.

Joey held up a finger and then dashed back into his room, turning down the stereo on his desk. He stayed there, flipping through loose pages laying there in a scattered mess. Drawings. Cassidy could just make out the image of a dog: a familiar-looking golden colored mastiff. If Joey'd drawn those, he'd gotten quite good since the last time they'd seen each other. And yet, the sight of the drawings made her feel queasy, for if the drawings were his, he hadn't yet moved on from what had happened to Lucky.

"You look different," she said standing in the doorway. Rose had exaggerated: He'd grown a little, but he was still pretty short for their age. His brown hair was long and covered his ears. His skin was paler than the previous year, as if he'd not been in the sun since school had let out in June.

"You too," he said over his shoulder. But he'd barely glanced at her.

"Can I come in?"

"Uh." Joey hesitated, not looking up.

Seconds passed, and Cassidy felt her face flush. "Oh, it's okay," she said before he could reply, waving her hands as if to clear away bad air. "Forget it." She didn't want to hear him say *no*. "I should bring my bags over to Tony's room."

"Good idea."

Cassidy smiled and then turned stiffly away. "Well, I hope you're feeling better now," she called over her shoulder.

"Better than what?" he answered.

Cassidy paused just around the corner. "Your mom said you weren't feeling well."

"Oh, no," Joey said, chuckling. "I just told her that so I wouldn't have to . . ." He trailed off, as if realizing what he'd been about to say. *So I wouldn't have to come with her to get you.*

Cassidy blanched. "Well, I'm really excited to be back," she squeaked out, tightening her lips so they wouldn't tremble.

"Me too." Joey's voice from within his bedroom.

She started down the hall, thinking of the notebook knocking against her spine. *The Book of Bad Things.* Levi Stanton, the neighbor who had given it to her, suggested during one particularly awful evening that if she researched and wrote down all the things that scared her, they might not seem so scary anymore. The notebook had become a catalogue of atrocities, a horrid list of *nastiness* from A to Z and back again. Natural disasters. Wars. Pandemics. Monsters. But this — this new version of Joey — left her feeling something different. Not simply *bad*; indescribable. And a little bit dizzy. "Let's hang out when I'm unpacked."

"Yeah," Joey said as the music swelled once more. "Maybe."

CASSIDY'S BOOK OF BAD THINGS, ENTRY #56:
ZOMBIES

Imagine a human face whose skin is peeling off in wide sheets so that you can see pinkish bone underneath. Imagine the eyes, bulging and pale, as if they're about to pop like balloons, as they catch sight of you. Imagine an unhinged jaw hanging at a crooked angle so that the mouth is drawn down into a jagged frown. Imagine that mouth creaking open, revealing broken teeth and a blackened, flapping tongue, as it comes closer, trying to bite.

Images like these terrified me a couple of nights ago when Janet and Benji invited me over to watch a video. The decaying zombies in the film freaked me out really bad. Nightmare bad. So I've done some research to help me sort out my thoughts. And what I've learned about them, the <u>truth</u> about zombies, might be even worse!

Most people think of zombies as these movie monsters, dead people risen from the grave to walk the earth with an unquenchable desire to feast on living flesh. I guess, in a way, this is what zombies are now, how we see them in theaters and on television screens with friends on Halloween. But zombies aren't only make-believe.

Some people believe that zombies are real — that they are human beings who've been poisoned by evil "witch doctors." The poison slows their hearts to an "undetectable rate" and the victims appear to be dead. Their families mourn and hold funerals and bury the poor people, even though they are secretly alive.

Later, after the poison wears off, the victim wakes up in the coffin! The witch doctor sneaks back to the cemetery and digs up the person. But the person is not the same as before. They are listless, unable to speak. They look pale, like a corpse, and move stiffly. These symptoms are long-lasting effects of the poison. The witch doctor takes the victim from the cemetery to his home where he keeps the "zombie" as a slave, to work and do whatever nefarious deeds the witch doctor requests.

A real zombie may look like the person they were before they were poisoned, but they're not. It's as though their souls have been stolen away, replaced by something new. Or by nothing at all.

Imagine that.

CHAPTER SIX

A SHORT WHILE LATER, Cassidy sat on Tony's mattress, staring out the open window toward the Tremonts' backyard. Since Rose had forgotten she was coming, Tony may have recently slept here. So Cassidy had stripped the sheets, located fresh ones in the linen closet in the hallway, and remade the bed, wiping at her eyes with the corners of the bedspread.

When Rose returned, she came upstairs and knocked on the closed bedroom door, but Cassidy called out that she was changing her clothes. She couldn't let anyone see her crying.

What if she wanted to go back to the city? How hard would it be to get in touch with her social worker to arrange for another bus ticket? If she left, what would she tell her friends Janet and Benji . . . or Levi Stanton? What would she do when Naomi, her mother, laughed at her, chiding her for thinking she was worth some rich family's time and money? And love.

Outside, an expanse of lawn sloped up toward a distinct line of trees where the hillside forest interrupted the neighborhood. One tree in particular caught Cassidy's attention — a tall oak that rose high above the house's roof, the roots of which came closer to the back patio than those of the other trees. This was the tree where the Tremonts had once leashed Lucky.

Something was moving by its base. An animal. Cassidy leaned toward the screen, catching a glimpse of what looked like dirty fur and tall haunches before the thing disappeared around the other side of the trunk.

A dog barked, brief and rough and angry. Cassidy flinched, unsure if the sound was real or only in her imagination, if it was nearby or far away. Rubbing goose bumps from her arms, she stood and backed away from the window. She didn't know why the sound disturbed her. She liked dogs. She often wished for one of her own. That could have been any of the neighborhood dogs, but there was something about the barking that reminded her of old Lucky.

Cassidy made her way down the hall, sneaking past Joey's closed door. Downstairs, Rose was busy in the kitchen, so Cassidy went out to the backyard, stepping cautiously toward the oak tree. She kept a wide berth, in case the thing she'd seen from the upstairs window was hiding behind the trunk. Slowly, she approached and placed her palm on the rough bark. A silvery loop had been screwed into the wood. This had been the link that held the end of Lucky's long leash, giving him free reign of the backyard. Cassidy touched the metal and flinched at its coldness. And before she realized what her mind was doing, she found herself thinking about that afternoon, almost one year ago, when everything had changed.

Cassidy and Joey had been bored. By that first week in August the previous year, it seemed as though they'd done everything they could do. However, there was one activity the two of them had steered clear of, a possibility they'd never talked about: visiting Joey's mysterious neighbor up the hill.

On the first night Cassidy had ever spent in Whitechapel, Joey had shared Ursula's story. Over the next two summers, Cassidy overheard his neighbors tell their own versions of Ursula Chambers's tale. The woman was a local legend. There were several things that most people agreed to be true, all of which had

occurred before Joey was even born. Ursula's elderly uncle Aidan
had owned the land on which Chase Estates now sat. When he'd
passed away, Ursula inherited the centuries-old farmhouse along
with everything in it. She'd arrived in Whitechapel, a whip of
Irish energy. Her thick brogue entertained folks whenever she'd
venture into town for an errand. Ursula was short and squat, with
a round, red face. Her hair was curly and gray, cut in a bob. Though
her blue eyes were small, almost swollen, they were the center of her
engaging and kind energy. She always wore a matching sweatshirt
and sweatpants. She seemed to have a pair in every color imagin-
able: pink, brown, yellow, fuchsia, turquoise, baby blue.

She'd been in the house for about a year before people noticed
a change. Her tone turned brusque and short. Where she'd once
been friendly to everyone in Whitechapel, she now cut them off,
unwilling to converse. Soon, she stopped coming into town. In
fact, she rarely left her house at all. The boys who delivered her
groceries and other supplies claimed that she demanded they leave
the bags at the bottom of her front steps. And she never tipped
them. When a sulfuric stench wafted through the thicket between
her house and the cul-de-sac, they figured she'd canceled her trash
pickup. Some theorized she was burning her garbage in her own
backyard.

Of course, the local kids grew curious. Some of them
approached the house to see if she would respond. She did — by
screaming at them. Yelling out from her darkened windows.
Threatening to make any trespassers sorry. Soon, she became a
pariah, the target of eggings, of small fires set in her driveway,
of the awful graffiti that now decorated all sides of the poor old
farmhouse. They started calling her The Hermit of Chase Estates.

Cassidy had been intrigued by the tales, but she also thought
they might actually be able to make a connection with Ursula, so
the previous summer, Cassidy had suggested they visit her. In the

city, Cassidy knew several elderly people — relatives of her classmates, even some of the neighbors in her building — who'd been
stuck, by circumstance and their own frail bodies, in their cramped
apartments. They were mostly just sad and lonely and had given up
on life in a way that was difficult for Cassidy, or any young person,
to understand. A few times, her neighbor Levi Stanton had invited
her to accompany him as he knocked on their secluded neighbors'
doors, with gifts of wine or cheese or chocolates. He loved talking
to them and hearing their stories, he explained to Cassidy later, not
only because they were often great inspiration for his books, but
also because of the looks on their faces when he said hello to them.
Cassidy wanted to see the same expression on Joey's secretive
neighbor's face.

The plan was simple. They'd march up to the house and knock
on the door and invite themselves in. Ursula couldn't be as bad as
everyone said. But Joey wasn't sure it was a good idea. What if she
attacked them? Cassidy laughed and suggested bringing Lucky
along. "For *luck*!" she'd said. When Joey continued to hang back,
she added, "What's the worst that could happen?"

CHAPTER SEVEN

THEY'D GONE THROUGH the woods. "We should come up from the back," Cassidy suggested, to avoid Ursula's view down her driveway. Joey stayed behind by a few feet, holding tightly to Lucky's leash. They trampled the brush, avoiding thickets of pricklier bushes and any reddish leaves.

Soon, the building appeared through the thinning trees. The house would have been quaint had it been maintained over the years. But now, its grayish brown color had been covered in spots of blackish green. Mildew or mold, something toxic and insidious, clung to the broken shingles. True to the tales, nasty words had been spray painted and carved into the sides of the house.

All of the window screens were covered in years of dust and dirt. Beyond, the glass itself looked as though it had been spattered with a thick sludge. The panes in the basement looked especially bad, some of them broken and padded with what looked like old curtains or blankets.

The backyard was barely a yard at all, mostly patches of bare ground covered in fallen acorns and pine needles, interspersed among plots of ragweed and several tall trees that drenched the place in ominous shadow.

"Wow," said Joey, coming up behind Cassidy. "It's like she's barricaded herself in there."

Cassidy shook her head. "We've got to help."

"What if she doesn't want any help?"

"Some people don't know they need help until they get it," said

Cassidy, stepping forward, pushing through some of the taller grass, her chin held high.

"Wait," Joey whispered. "Be careful. She's probably watching us."

Cassidy imagined Ursula hunched at a cracked windowsill: a plump little woman dressed in a fluorescent green running suit. Cassidy had seen scarier things inside her own apartment back in the city. She lifted a hand and waved. Pausing, she scanned each of the windows that faced the backyard, but she saw no movement. "Let's try the side door."

Joey sighed in dismay, but he and Lucky continued beside her. Suddenly, the mastiff pulled forward so hard, Joey lost his grip on the leash. The dog bounded toward the base of the house, barking and sniffing at the splintered glass.

Joey chased after Lucky, calling out for him to *Heel!* Lucky didn't heed him, tugging at a piece of blanket that was sticking out past the broken glass. Cassidy froze where she stood about a dozen yards from the farmhouse. Something was moving behind the screen right above the dog. A creaking noise split the air as the sash lifted. A pale face emerged from the darkness.

Ursula's message was brief but thunderous. "Get out of here!"

Joey leapt for Lucky's collar, trying to pull the dog away from the window. "We're sorry, Mrs. Chambers!" he called up to her.

"I don't care if you're bleeding to death. Get out of my yard! Now!"

Cassidy simply stood there. Ursula didn't need help, didn't want help, wouldn't know what help was if it came up and poked her in the eye. Cassidy's fingers went numb, her neck tingled. The ground tilted and her body felt like it was shrinking. It was how she'd felt back in the city, whenever she had an "episode" at school and ended up at the nurse's office.

She gripped the straps of her backpack as the world began to spin, and the only thing she could think to do was run.

A few minutes later, Joey met her in the Tremonts' backyard, dragging Lucky with him. By that time, Cassidy had caught her breath, had regained feeling in her hands and feet and neck. But Joey's face was red, his hair slick with sweat. His mouth was twisted with anger. "Thanks," he said, clipping the leash to the oak tree. "Great idea."

"I'm sorry," she said quietly. "I didn't think she would be like that."

"Why not? Because you're so special?"

Lucky was still excited. He leapt up on Joey, knocking him against the tree.

Cassidy noticed a piece of blanket sticking out of the dog's mouth. She reached out to pull it away, but Lucky growled at her. She blushed and then brushed herself off. "I don't think that." She remembered the notebook in her backpack, her *Book of Bad Things*. Levi had told her that writing down the things that scared her, naming them, facing them, would help with the panic attacks. Why would Ursula Chambers have hidden herself away inside her house if she too didn't harbor a collection of fears? "I just thought that I might have had some good advice for her." Joey shrugged, lifted an eyebrow. But Cassidy hadn't shared the secret of her book with him. So she only shook her head and apologized again.

Finally, he rolled his eyes. "Goofball. I guess that was pretty exciting anyway."

As Rose called to them that dinner was almost ready, they left Lucky at the tree. He lapped greedily at the water in his bowl. The scrap of blanket lay a few inches away.

❖

Now, Cassidy stepped away from the oak, eyeing the empty hook where they'd attached the leash. The leash had been connected to the collar around Lucky's neck. She shuddered, leaning toward the shadows of the forest. She searched for the place where Joey had marked the dog's grave, a disruption of earth, but dead brush littered the ground, hiding the marker.

Something moved through the trees up the hill. Cassidy crept closer. This animal seemed large enough to be a deer. But when she squinted to catch a better glimpse of it, it was gone. She thought of the thing she'd seen from Tony's window minutes earlier, the dirty fur, the tall haunches. It had looked like Lucky. A growl came from the scrub brush. It *was* a dog. And it didn't sound friendly. Cassidy held her breath, crossing her arms, hoping she was as invisible to it as it was to her. She was determined to get back to the house without making a sound, but then a hand fell on her shoulder and she screamed.

CHAPTER EIGHT

"Whoa!" said a high-pitched, unfamiliar voice.

Cassidy jumped and spun, flinging her arms out. The girl who'd been standing behind her retreated several feet, covering her face with her hands, fingers splayed.

"Sorry!" Cassidy shouted. "I'm sorry. I wasn't going to hit you. I'm just . . . a little jumpy."

The girl stood frozen for a moment. She was Cassidy's height, but thinner, her arms like bare bones, her elbows protruding like knobs. Her skin was so pale it was almost translucent. At the sides of her head, blue veins branched, disappearing into her long, straight, pitch-black hair. She was dressed in black cargo shorts and a black T-shirt decorated with a small pink skull decal on the chest. Her worn-out All Star sneakers were also black, as were her socks, which she had pulled up over her knees. "I should know better than to sneak up on people. Especially back here. *I'm* sorry."

Back here? What was that supposed to mean?

"My name is Ping," said the girl. "I live on that side of the Tremonts." She nodded in the opposite direction of the Chambers house. "My family moved in last year, just before school started. You're the girl who's staying with them this summer, right? We must have missed each other by a couple weeks back then."

"I'm Cassidy." Dropping her tensed shoulders, she waved, a flip of several fingers.

Ping smiled and then chuckled and waved back the same way.

She watched Cassidy observe her outfit and seemed to read her mind. "My nickname at school is *Spooky*," she said and shrugged.

"I'm not *really* spooky though, I don't think; not most of the time. It's just that I'm not interested in the same things as a lot of other girls. You know: kittens or sports or being BFFs and writing notes back and forth all day long. I don't really care what people say, and as long as I have a book with me, I'm okay."

"Huh," said Cassidy. "Me too." *Sort of.* She tightened the straps of her backpack, feeling the weight of her notebook shift against her spine. "What are you reading now?" Cassidy asked.

Ping's hand moved to a cargo pocket that seemed especially full. "It's a book about ancient Egypt. Actually, this one is about what they believed happens to you after you die, you know, the rituals they did to prepare you for the afterlife." Her face lit up. "Did you know that, back then, the Egyptians took out all of the dead person's organs and kept them in jars? They even had these long hooks that they stuck up a person's nose to pull out his brains! So cool."

"Yeah, I think I read about that somewhere too," said Cassidy, clutching her arms. "Very . . . cool." Strange that this girl didn't think of herself as *actually* spooky. She seemed to be the very definition of the word.

"And they mummified cats! I saw one in a museum in New York once. Isn't that *so* weird?"

Cassidy glanced over her shoulder behind the oak tree. She remembered why she'd come to the backyard in the first place — the large creature she'd seen moving through the shadows. All this talk about the dead, and now dead animals, was making her lightheaded. Lucky was buried somewhere back there.

Ping gasped, looking where Cassidy had focused her attention. "You were here when it happened, weren't you?"

"When what happened?"

"The accident with the Tremonts' dog."

Cassidy held her breath for a moment. "Lucky. Yeah. I was here. Joey never believed it was an accident."

Ping smiled sadly. "Trust me, I've heard him tell the story at school plenty of times. Kids are starting to call him *spooky* too. And worse things."

"Worse things? Like what?"

"Like *crazy*."

The previous summer, on the day that Cassidy suggested they make contact with Ursula Chambers, she and Joey had left the dog outside when they'd gone in for dinner. Later, when Joey opened the back door to bring Lucky in, the dog didn't stir from his spot near the oak. Not even when Joey approached. Mr. Tremont rushed the dog to the local animal hospital, but it was too late. Cassidy had held Joey's hand as the doctor delivered the horrible news. She'd been too much in shock even to cry. The strange part, though, was what the vet had pulled out of Lucky's mouth: A scrap of cloth had been lodged in there. The poor thing had choked on it. Only when the family got home did Cassidy realize where the scrap had come from. It was the same piece of blanket that Lucky had torn away from the broken basement window at Ursula's house.

Later that night, Mr. Tremont dug a deep hole back beyond the oak and placed Lucky's body at the bottom. In the morning, the family gathered to pay their respects. When it was Joey's turn to speak, he said something that shocked everyone, especially Cassidy. His face red and his voice shaking, he claimed that Ursula Chambers had done this. The old Hermit of Chase Estates had left her house for just long enough to cross her yard and kill his dog. Joey begged his father to go to the police, to file charges, to do *something*, but Dennis only answered by hugging his son close and whispering, *It was an accident, son. It's over.*

"Crazy," echoed Cassidy. "Why *crazy*?"

Ping squinted at her. "Haven't you two spoken since last fall?"

Cassidy tensed. "Not really. I guess we've both been busy this year." She shrugged, trying to hide her blush by stepping into the shade of the oak.

"So he never told you that someone stole his dog?"

Cassidy's mouth snapped open. "*What?* How?"

"Dug up the body and took it away. Joey flipped out. He insisted Ursula did it. He couldn't prove it, but he said he knew it was her. The police were involved and everything, but they didn't have any evidence to get a search warrant for the farmhouse. Not that they would have found Lucky in there anyway, what with all the crud they've been pulling out for the past few days."

"What kind of person would do such a thing?" Cassidy asked, making a mental note for a *Book of Bad Things* entry: *grave robbing.*

"It doesn't stop there. Last December, Joey started telling stories about seeing Lucky."

"*Seeing* the dead dog?"

Ping nodded. "Joey said that he saw him out here by this tree, wandering through the woods." Cassidy's arms erupted with gooseflesh. Ping went on, "He said he sometimes heard the click-clack of the dog's claws following him through the hallways at school."

"That's awful," Cassidy whispered, thinking of Joey alone in his room, flipping through his sketches.

"Supposedly, his parents got tired of all his stories. . . . Well, tired or scared. My mom says Joey's seeing some sort of doctor now. He's been pretty quiet lately." Cassidy wiped at her eyes. Ping went even paler than she'd been before. She reached out to touch Cassidy's shoulder. "I'm sorry! I didn't mean to —"

Voices drifted from the Tremonts' open kitchen window. "I don't care!" It was Joey. "You can't make me! Why don't *you* go outside and look for her? You're the one who brought her back again."

Ping grabbed Cassidy's arm and led her behind the oak. "Don't listen," she whispered.

"Is he talking about me?" Cassidy asked.

"I don't know," said Ping, though her expression said the opposite. "He's never been very nice to me, though, not since I moved in. He keeps to himself. Pretends I don't exist. The funny thing is, I'm like the one person who *wants* to hear his ghost-dog stories."

Cassidy frowned. *You're the one who brought her back again. . . .* Who else could he have been talking about? It was like a kickball to the stomach. "When I knew him," she said, "he was always really fun. . . . He was like my first best guy friend."

It suddenly all made sense. The delay in hearing from her social worker about being placed with the Tremonts this year; Joey actually *was* mad at her for what happened the previous summer. So mad that he hadn't wanted to see her again. If it hadn't been for Rose, Cassidy would have remained in Brooklyn, ignored by her mother. Now, she'd be ignored by Joey instead.

"I have to get out of here," said Cassidy, turning and walking toward the street.

"Okay," said Ping, following. "Where should we go?"

We?

Cassidy paused, feeling a momentary sense of relief. She turned and stared at the pale skinny girl standing behind her. Ping tucked a long strand of hair behind her left ear and then pressed her lips in a sad smile. So Cassidy wouldn't have to be alone after all. Not this afternoon, anyway. Still, she answered with a huff. "I wanna see what's happening over by the Hermit's house."

Cassidy's Book of Bad Things, Entry #15:
DEATH

I've heard a lot of people saying lately that death is a natural occurrence. That it's a good thing. That even though it's sad when it happens, it does happen to everyone. That it'll happen to me one day, a long time from now. But how can anyone be sure about that last part? About when?

This girl in my class named Jackie Spencer died last week. A livery cab hit her when she was walking home from school with her mom. An accident.

There's nothing natural about what happened to Jackie. She was my age. And she had so much life left, just like me. I hope.

I saw my friends crying. And their parents too. I got this horrible headache and a pain in my stomach that made me not want to eat. They say that these feelings will go away. It just takes time. But it hurts so much, I can't believe that.

So I don't think that death is a good thing. I think it's a bad thing. It's one of the most horrible, bad, and unfair things I can think of in this whole stupid world. And I'm putting it in this notebook because I want Death to Know I understand. People can say what they want, but I Know the truth. I can feel it.

CHAPTER NINE

STANDING AT THE END of the cul-de-sac, the two girls watched in awe as the cleaning crew filled the two overflowing Dumpsters. Most of what they brought out was already bagged and tied, but there were a few items — furniture, open cardboard boxes, pieces of framed artwork — that were simply tossed on top of the pile. Some of it had spilled onto the gravel driveway.

Cassidy recognized several of the Tremonts' neighbors who'd gathered in groups around the asphalt circle. Rumors swirled too quickly to catch all of them. Supposedly, another large bin was on its way. The crew hoped to be finished by evening but there was so much junk inside that old farmhouse, no one was sure how long the clean-up would take.

As the sun beat down on the girls, sweat beaded on their foreheads, and they told each other their own stories, where they'd come from, where they wanted to go. Ping had grown up in a city too, though hers had been on the West Coast and not nearly as large or intimidating as New York. Her twin brothers were a few years younger than she. Her parents were both professors at different universities in the area. Ping liked the change here, especially since New Jersey had its own particular brand of *peculiar* — and a whole magazine dedicated to that fact. In the pages of *Strange State*, Ping had read about rinky-dink roadside attractions (Insect World! Haunted Mini-Golf!), abandoned highways, even a few ghost towns. She promised Cassidy that she'd share a few copies with her soon. And though Cassidy was happy for the distraction, she couldn't stop thinking of what she'd overheard Joey say inside the Tremonts' kitchen.

Was Lucky's death last summer really her fault? Should she apologize? Beg Joey's forgiveness? If Joey believed Lucky's ghost was haunting him, maybe he wasn't thinking properly. Maybe he just needed space. Then she thought of what she'd seen in the woods. The thing moving between the trees. And the sound of barking.

She glanced at Ping, who seemed intrigued by the heap in the driveway. "You don't believe Joey, do you?"

"About what?" Ping asked.

"That his dog is a ghost now."

"Of course I do," Ping answered. "Why would he have made up a story like that? It only seems to upset his parents. Unless he *wants* to upset his parents."

Cassidy watched Ping's eyes for a sign that she was kidding around — a squint, a glimmer of a hidden laugh — but Ping's face was open and friendly. "Say the dog really *is* a ghost," Cassidy whispered. "What if the ghost blames someone for what happened to it? What if Lucky has been waiting for that *someone* to return to Whitechapel, so he can get his revenge?"

Ping chuckled. "And you're that someone?" she said, not believing, not understanding.

Cassidy burned with embarrassment. "I saw something out by that tree. An animal. It was big."

"You're serious," said Ping, dropping her smile. "How could you have been responsible for what happened to Joey's dog?"

Cassidy sighed. The girls sat on the nearby curb. Then she told Ping the story, her version of it.

When Cassidy had finished, Ping said simply, "You were only trying to do something good."

"Yeah, but something bad happened because of it."

"Doesn't matter. Ghost dogs don't seek revenge on people who don't deserve it." Ping smiled, as if her statement were a well-known fact. "And *you* don't deserve it."

"Joey thinks I do."

"Then Joey's an idiot. And you can hang out with me this summer instead."

Cassidy smiled in spite of herself.

A commotion arose from the crowd. The girls stood and backed away from the gravel driveway. They watched as a large man barreled toward the street from the Dumpster. His belly bounced over the hem of his green plaid pants. Rivulets of sweat dripped down his bald head. Under his arm, he clutched what looked like a fuzzy red fox. The animal's face was serene, frozen, but it looked like it might turn and bite him. If the man dropped the fox and if it ran, it might attack. Cassidy stumbled. Ping caught her. As the man came closer, the fox remained still — its feet were attached to a wooden plank.

"It's dead," Ping whispered. "Stuffed."

"Stuffed with what?" Cassidy asked.

"Sawdust. Haven't you ever seen taxidermy before?"

Cassidy had not. "That man's taking Ursula's things?"

"Mr. Chase. Yeah. That's why everyone's standing out here, I guess, hoping to catch a glimpse of some treasure." Ping held out her hands to indicate the crowd. "It's all going to the dump anyhow."

"But he's taking it home?" said Cassidy. "I wouldn't want any of that old stuff in my house."

"That's what her family thought too. Supposedly, they're all overseas. Ireland, I think. They're the ones who hired the cleaning crew. They also sold the house back to Mr. Chase, the man who built this whole neighborhood. He's the *Chase* in Chase Estates."

Ping whispered this next part. "My mom says he's super rich. Thinks he owns this town. I heard he wants to fix up the farmhouse. Turn it into an ultra-modern mini-mansion or something. So I guess we'll be getting new neighbors sometime soon. Wonder if anyone will tell them who lived here before they moved in."

The man in the plaid pants, Mr. Chase himself, nearly ran the girls over as he crossed into the cul-de-sac. "Watch it," he said, wheezing in the heat with the weight of the fox under his arm. Then he called out, Cassidy assumed, to someone he knew standing amongst the crowd. "Found another one! These will pull in a pretty penny at the Hudson Auction next month. This Ursula lady was one weird old miser. Lucky for us, eh?" As he said the words, a cold gust of wind blew through the trees, shaking loose some high, dead branches that were stretched out over the street. One of them crashed to the ground, hitting the asphalt where Mr. Chase had just passed. The branch seemed to explode into several dozen brittle pieces and the crowd collectively gasped. Mr. Chase jumped and turned around. After a moment, he laughed, holding the fox above his head, as if showing it to Ursula's old house. "Mine now, sweetheart!" he bellowed. "You snooze, you lose!"

Cassidy and Ping glanced uneasily at each other. That was no way to speak to the dead.

CHAPTER TEN

LATER, AFTER THE SUN was low in the sky, Ping's mother called for her to come inside and clean up for dinner. The girls said good-bye with the hope of seeing each other again soon, and Cassidy made her way back to the Tremonts' house. Dennis's BMW was parked in the driveway and his daughter Deb's Taurus was in front of it, its engine still steaming and clicking in the open garage.

Cassidy didn't want to go back into the house just yet, so she perched on the wicker chair on the front porch and flipped through her notebook, finding the last blank page, and filling it with the little she knew of grave robbers. She'd have to look up more about the subject on Rose's laptop that evening if she had a chance. She supposed that what Mr. Chase and the others had done that afternoon had been a type of grave robbing too. His laugh echoed in her memory, and she grimaced thinking of his prize fox. She secretly hoped it woke up and bit him.

"Cassie!" a voice called from the street. "You're here!"

Cassidy looked up and noticed the boy from the supermarket waving at the edge of the lawn. Hal. "Hey!" She waved. "Yup, I made it . . . back." She'd almost said *home*.

"I can see that," he called out. "Hey, is there any good stuff left up at the Hermit's place?"

Cassidy remembered their conversation. He'd been waiting to get off his shift so he could come scrounge like the rest of them. She shrugged, lifting her hands in an I-don't-know gesture.

"Wish me luck!" he said.

"Good luck," Cassidy called out, as the boy walked on.

"Who you talking to?" Joey was standing behind her just inside the screen door.

She flinched. How long had he been watching her? "Your old babysitter. Hal."

"Well, my mom wanted me to tell you that she put some appetizers out. My dad's got some burgers on the grill out back."

"Everyone's sitting down to dinner?"

"Everyone else is. I'm not really hungry," said Joey. He turned around and disappeared into the shadows behind the screen door.

Cassidy sat at the picnic table on the back patio, pushing a pile of cold bean salad from one side of her plate to the other, her stomach feeling tight and too small to fit anything inside. It was the opposite of what Cassidy had regularly experienced only a year ago when she'd stuffed herself silly at every meal.

Dennis and Deb were seated beside her, talking about their days. Dennis Tremont was tall and thin, though he appeared broader when in his navy lawyer suit than in his current costume, a faded concert tee and black jeans. His hair was gray, which made him look a little older than he actually was, but slightly scruffy and handsome, like the hipster dads she'd seen in certain Brooklyn neighborhoods. Deb was obviously his daughter — they had the same sharp nose and wide, intelligent eyes. But Deb also had her mother's long neck and pale skin. Her dark auburn hair fell in effortless curls to her shoulders, which were bare except for the thin straps of a summery floral dress. Cassidy had never realized how much Deb looked like Joey. But Joey wasn't around for comparison; he'd already gone upstairs to his bedroom.

After a moment of silence, which Cassidy hadn't noticed, Rose reached out and took her hand. "I'm very sorry I forgot to pick you up today. I've got lots planned for the next couple weeks. I swear, I'll make it up to you."

Cassidy wore a tiny smile, answering in a small voice, "You already have."

"Tomorrow morning, you and Joey are taking an art class at the college. Sound like fun?"

"Totally!" Cassidy forced herself to sound excited. She wanted badly to tell Rose about the conversation she'd overheard earlier that afternoon. But as the light grew purple around them and the tree frogs began their familiar and lovely chorus, she realized that she should probably keep Rose and Dennis and Deb out of whatever was happening between her and Joey. There was so much more going on with him than any of them probably understood.

The day hadn't been all bad. She'd made a new friend, after all.

In the kitchen, Cassidy scraped her plate into the trash bin. She wondered what Ping was doing next door. Possibly, she was reading one of those magazines she'd mentioned. *Strange State*? Cassidy thought maybe tomorrow they could call up someone in the editor's office and tell them about the Hermit of Chase Estates and the junk that everyone had pulled out of her house, or about Lucky, the ghost dog that was haunting the woods nearby. Or maybe, Cassidy thought, she'd add these odd things to her own little journal.

Later, after presenting her gifts to the Tremonts — a bag of chocolate-covered potato chips from an expensive store on Atlantic Avenue and a small cheesecake from a famous Brooklyn bakery — she climbed the stairs to Tony's bedroom, *her* bedroom for now, thinking of what Levi Stanton had said about the nature of what scares us. The first step in conquering fear is recognizing where it's coming from. Cassidy had begun her *Bad Things* journal with this idea in mind. Stepping into the darkness beyond her host-brother's closed door, she made the decision that the name *Joey Tremont* would never go into her book. She would not allow him to become a *Bad Thing*, no matter how hard he tried to make her believe the opposite. They'd been friends once. How hard could it be to make that happen again?

CHAPTER ELEVEN

IN THE CITY, at night, when Cassidy slept on her little couch, she could hear the trains of the subway as they passed underground several blocks away. Sometimes the weight of the train would vibrate her entire neighborhood. Often, these vibrations would catch something in Cassidy's apartment — a picture frame hanging loosely, a couple glasses touching in the sink's drying rack, a piece of furniture sitting just-so on the slightly slanted wood flooring — and release a faint but obnoxious rattle. The noise never lasted long enough for Cassidy to find its source on the first try. And so she would wait fifteen minutes for the next train to pass, to send out its vibrations, and the rattle would come again.

It was like a game, though an unpleasant one — every passing tremor leading Cassidy closer to the offending object until finally she'd zero in on it. She'd shift that frame on the wall, or separate the glasses by the sink, or kick at the chair or bureau or table that had somehow, by pure chance, ended up in the exact wrong position. Then, if all went well, she'd crawl back underneath her blanket to capture a few more hours of sleep before dawn.

It was such a *city* type of annoyance, that when Cassidy was woken by a similar rattle that first night back in Whitechapel, she opened her eyes into darkness and panicked that the whole day had been a dream, that she was still in Brooklyn, huddled on her hot little couch. But soon Tony's room — *her* room — took shape, and she clutched at the soft sheets she'd taken from the hall closet only that afternoon.

Above, the ceiling fan spun at mid speed, creating a soft din that almost drowned out all other noise. Almost. Something was rattling close by, just like in the city when the subway growled through its underground passages.

Cassidy sat up. She straightened her T-shirt and shorts. She stood still and craned her neck, listening. The vibration must have been tiny or very far away, because she could not feel it against her bare feet. Tony's bedroom was above the garage and was large enough that it looked out on both the front and back yards. There was usually a cooling cross-breeze after the sun went down. What if the breeze itself was the culprit?

But the rattle sounded as though it were coming from beside the window facing the street. As she neared the sill, she thought that the bookcase there must be rubbing ever-so-slightly against the wall. She pulled the wooden case away and the rattle stopped. She listened to the quiet night to see if the rattle came again from somewhere else. But it did not. The house itself must have been trembling. But why? How? A couple years ago, she'd felt the earthquake that hit the city; her desk at school had rocked back and forth like she was on a boat. But this had been different.

Cassidy heard a soft humming. Low and barely perceptible. If she hadn't been standing by the window, she'd never have noticed it. The humming was not melodious; more like the chanting of the Buddhist monks that Mrs. Mendez had played for her world-music class earlier that year. Cassidy listened closely. There were layers inside of it. Different notes. Discordant. Difficult. Like a song the moon might sing while dreaming.

She imagined Joey in the next room, wondering if he was asleep. Her heart sped up at the thought of confronting him the next day. . . . Not *confronting*, exactly. Talking. Acknowledging that something strange was going on between them. She hadn't quite picked out the words she'd use, and in fact, had only hours earlier fallen asleep scripting fantasy responses to all the ways he might answer her questions.

Cassidy had just pulled herself away from the bookcase and the window when another sound echoed into the night. Something was moving out on the street, as if bits of gravel were caught underneath a heavy object that someone was dragging up the road toward the cul-de-sac.

Kneeling at the window's edge, Cassidy leaned forward until her face met the taut screen. Though the half-moon had already dipped below the horizon, she could make out a dark shadow, human shaped, limping up the road. The figure wore a sort of shift or dress or nightgown. She moved stiffly, as though severely injured.

Cassidy grasped the window ledge, digging her fingernails into the wood, pinching the tips of her fingers so that she knew she wasn't dreaming.

Why would someone be out so late, especially if they were hurt?

She wanted to run out into the hallway and pound on Joey's door, to make him see what she was seeing, but she was frightened that the walker would hear her, peer up at her, see her face. That would be a bad, bad thing.

Screee. Screee.

The sound grated at her eardrums as the figure moved farther into the cul-de-sac, into the darkness of the trees that surrounded the old farmhouse where Ursula Chambers had died.

When the shuffling sound was an echo in her memory, Cassidy stood, moving slowly backward toward her bed, keeping the street in sight. Then, just as she reached the mattress, a barking exploded the new quiet. Short. Harsh. Angry. Like the barking she'd heard that afternoon coming from the backyard.

Another figure, the same shape and size that Lucky had been before he'd died, followed in the path of the first one, dragging its hind leg before it too disappeared into the darkness of the dead-end street.

CASSIDY'S BOOK OF BAD THINGS, ENTRY #30:
SLEEPWALKING

I've read that you should never try to wake anyone who is walking in her sleep. To do so could be harmful to her. The thing is, I can't find any information about what kind of harm. Will the sleepwalker immediately go insane? Will her brain explode? Will she lose her memory, or even worse, will she slip deeper into sleep and never wake up again? It all sounds silly to me. Impossible.

I think sleepwalking is probably more dangerous if you leave the person alone.

Janet and Benji told me a story about their teenage cousin, Flora, who lives on Long Island. Flora has been sleepwalking since she was really young. It started out kind of cute. Flora's mother would find her going through her closet in the middle of the night. With the lights off. When Flora's mother asked what she was doing, Flora said she was looking for an outfit to wear to her birthday party. Her birthday wasn't for another six months or so.

Another time, Flora woke up while standing in the kitchen. The smoke alarm had gone off because she'd put a jar of peanut butter in the microwave for five minutes. The peanut butter had turned crispy and black. After the initial fright of being awoken by the alarm, the rest of the family came downstairs and opened the windows to clear the smoke. Everyone had a good laugh.

But as Flora grew older, her family began to worry about the sleepwalking. Flora started leaving the house in the night.

She'd wake in the morning, her feet muddy and plastered with pieces of grass, with no memory of going outdoors. Flora's mother responded by putting chain locks on all the doors.

It didn't work.

One night, Flora's mother woke up to find flashing lights out in the street. Someone was knocking on the front door. The police had found Flora way out on the Long Island Expressway, wandering in her nightgown along the shoulder of the highway. She'd almost been hit by a car.

Flora's in some sort of sleep study now at a local hospital. She's under constant observation. She might even be taking medicine. According to Janet and Benji, her doctors say she'll grow out of it someday. Until then, they're not taking any chances.

I'm just thankful that Flora's family cares enough to try to wake her up when she's in trouble. Can you imagine what might happen if her mother wasn't around to help?

I sure can.

CHAPTER TWELVE

THE NEXT MORNING, Cassidy woke to find that she had only a half hour to shower, devour a small breakfast of toast and jam, brush her teeth, and get dressed before they had to be on their way to the art class. She was so frantic that the previous night's events sat squarely in the back of her mind.

After saying a quick hello to both Dennis and Deb, who were also running out the door, Cassidy tossed her backpack into the backseat of Rose's hatchback and rolled in beside it. Rose sped through the hills with the windows down and the stereo turned up, playing an old Joni Mitchell album, nudging at Joey playfully every now and again to sing along with her. Cassidy felt a strange emptiness as she watched him lean his head against the window, obviously wanting nothing to do with what must have been an old ritual. Even though she didn't know any of the words and could only discern bits of the melody, Cassidy opened her mouth and did her best to sing backup. Rose glanced over her shoulder, smiled and then held out a hand, palm up, toward the backseat. Cassidy gave her some skin, smacking her host-mother's hand loud enough to rustle Joey momentarily from his reverie.

The campus of Western New Jersey State College was all green fields and brick buildings connected by sprawling concrete paths. Rose walked with Cassidy and Joey through the brightly lit halls of the art school until they came to what appeared to be the correct classroom. Inside, the tables were arranged in a circle, with a single desk in the center. Most of the tables were already occupied with other kids their age, all chatting with one another. A bearded man who looked young enough to be a college student welcomed them inside. He was dressed in a simple white collared shirt and paint-splattered khaki pants. He pointed Cassidy and Joey to a table by the far window. Joey huffed as he slid into his seat. Cassidy pressed her lips together and reminded herself that Joey would not become a *Bad Thing*. Maybe she'd have time during class to tell him what she'd seen the previous night. That might change everything between them, reforge their bond. Rose waved good-bye from the doorway and mouthed that she'd meet them out by the car when the class was over.

The young-looking man introduced himself as Vic. He explained that he was a graduate student at the college. On each table, he'd already set up a tray of pencils, erasers, and a few large scraps of thick poster board. Vic told them that since they were already intermediate-level students, he was skipping all the boring "talky-stuff" so they could jump right into drawing.

Vic asked that one person from each table bring something up to place on the desk in the center of the room. This pile would be the subject of the day. Some of the other kids took off a shoe, a hat, brought up a book, a wad of tissue, the wrapper from a hastily eaten breakfast snack. "What should we put up there?" Cassidy asked. Joey stared at the table and shrugged. Squaring her jaw, she got up and placed her backpack on the table. But as she sat down next to Joey again, she wished she'd removed her notebook first. She needed it closer now.

"Thank you, volunteers," Vic said, heading to the still life, spreading out the items, leaning them against one another in a dynamic way. "Let's get started." He turned on a stereo that sat on a shelf by his desk. Quiet, ambient music filled the room, the sounds of bells and chimes and softly plucked guitar strings.

Watching from the corner of her eye, after a few minutes, Cassidy noticed the lines on Joey's page coming into a discernible shape; her own drawing looked like a blob of goop sitting on a cold stone slab. Vic strolled around the circle, commenting on various drawings, making suggestions. Cassidy was sure that when he came by her table, he wouldn't be able to contain his laughter. But she didn't care about that right now.

Joey was focused on what he was doing.

"That's really good," she whispered.

"Thanks."

Cassidy sighed. "Is something wrong?"

"Nope. I'm fine."

"That's cool." Seconds ticked by, every moment like a little bomb going off. "Hey, remember when your mom used to make us go up the hill in your backyard to find different shaped leaves? And we'd bring them back to her and we'd do rubbings of them with crayons? And that one time we picked poison ivy and she totally freaked out and made us both take showers?" She pushed out a laugh that sounded like a bark. Several students glanced up at her. "This kind of art is totally different than that, isn't it? It's harder. Maybe it's 'cause we're older now." Joey breathed heavily, hunching over his paper. Cassidy waited for a response until her skin felt like it was on fire. "Listen," she said finally. "I know you're mad at me." In her mind, she heard his voice from yesterday, wafting out into the backyard — the argument he'd had with his mother about her.

"I'm not mad at you," Joey said, turning to look at her. His eyebrows were screwed up in anger.

"But you've been . . . acting different."

"Things *are* different this summer." Joey pressed against the page so hard, his pencil broke. "Fart," he whispered, reaching for an eraser and a small sharpener.

Cassidy blinked, a gurgle of laughter creeping up her throat. Joey had always made the funniest exclamations. Maybe he wasn't so different now after all. She bit her bottom lip so that she wouldn't smile. "I just wanted to let you know that I'm sorry. About what happened." He groaned, and Cassidy's humor was released like air from a popped balloon. "I know it was my fault. If I hadn't suggested we go over to Ursula's house —"

"Forget it," Joey said harshly. "I don't want to talk about that."

Cassidy nodded slightly. A burning sensation crept up from her stomach. "Well . . . if you ever do want to talk about it, I'm here. I understand."

"Right."

"Yesterday, I noticed the drawings of him on your desk. You've been thinking about him a lot. I have been too. But I've also been thinking about you."

"And *now* we're supposed to be thinking about this." He opened his hands over his page, presenting his work as if he were in an art gallery.

Cassidy blushed, and as she turned back to her own drawing, she felt her hand shake. She placed the pencil carefully on the desk. "So, even though I'm apologizing," Cassidy whispered, those old feelings crawling up her spine, knocking the room off-kilter, "and even though I am really, *really* sorry for what happened, you're telling me you just don't care? That I can't do anything to make things better?"

Joey closed his eyes and shook his head. "All I'm saying is that you have no idea what I've been dealing with since you left last year. None. Nobody does. And all of the apologies in the world, from you or my mom or dad — even from Ursula Chambers herself — none of it would change how I feel. *Okay?*"

"Okay," Cassidy said. Her fingertips tingled, pins and needles caressing her arms, working their way up to her shoulders and neck. Her throat felt tight. She stuck out her bottom jaw, as if it were a lever to keep tears away.

Vic passed by their table. He praised Joey for his line-work. When his gaze fell upon Cassidy's drawing, he bit his lip and nodded. "Keep going," he said. "I like this." Not what she'd expected to hear. It made her feel good. Strong. So once the teacher had moved on, Cassidy worked up the nerve to say what was really on her mind.

"I know you've seen Lucky." She squeezed out the words. Joey froze. A statue. Clay. Dried and fired. So much easier to talk to this way. "I believe you because I've seen him too."

CHAPTER THIRTEEN

"WHAT ARE YOU TALKING ABOUT?" Joey said, whipping his head toward her, a bright blaze in his eyes.

"I saw Lucky," Cassidy answered. "Last night." A couple kids at the next table glared at her. All this talking must be annoying them, but she finally had Joey's attention. Cassidy pretended to concentrate on her paper, tracing some of the lines she'd already put down. She lowered her voice and shared what she'd seen in the middle of the night. As she spoke, she glanced up a few times to find his gaze glued to her. She went on about hearing the rattling sound, about the strange humming, about seeing the figure limping up the street toward the cul-de-sac. About the dog that followed.

When she finished, Joey's face went blank. Then he stood, knocking his stool over. It tumbled to the linoleum floor, clanging out into the otherwise quiet classroom, a strange accompaniment to the music emanating from Vic's speakers. He tossed his pencil at his paper, marking it through with a severe dark line and then he bolted for the door. Seconds later, he'd disappeared into the hallway.

Everyone was looking at Cassidy. She scooted her chair back, too shocked to speak. "Everything okay?" Vic asked, easing toward her.

She stood and crossed to the center of the room, pausing before the still life display. She reached for her backpack, and then realized that if she snatched it away, she'd ruin the assignment for the rest of the class. But she would not leave the bag here, not with the notebook inside. Her stomach clenched. She didn't have time to be careful. Joey was who-knew-where thinking who-knew-what about her.

"This is . . . mine," she whispered as she lifted the backpack from the table, disrupting the still life. The hat and the shoe fell to the floor. Vic's jaw dropped in shock, and he choked out a weird croaking sound. Cassidy hastily reset the objects. "Sorry. I just really have to . . ."

Everyone stared at her, their eyes blazing with uncomprehending fury.

She rushed to the door, clasping the backpack's strap in her sweat-slicked palms, and slipped out into the hall as quietly as possible.

She found Joey sitting on the floor in front of the boys' room in the art center lobby. His head was tucked between his knees. His shoulders hitched and shook. When she realized that he was crying, she ground the toe of her sneaker into the floor, preparing to spin around, leave him alone. She wasn't used to seeing other people cry, especially not boys. Especially not Joey. She didn't know what to do, so she stood in the hall and stared at the floor.

After a minute, he said, "You're being creepy."

Her sneaker squealed against the tile and Cassidy cringed. No running away now. "I just wanted to make sure you didn't, like, jump out a window or anything."

Joey sniffed sharply. She couldn't tell if he'd just laughed or if he'd scoffed at her bad joke. He wiped his nose with his wrist.

"Are you coming back to class?" Cassidy asked.

"Uh, no." He scrunched his feet closer to his butt and squeezed his ankles. "It's a nice thought, what you said. About last night. But you really don't need to make up stories just to make me feel better."

"I didn't make anything up. I really saw someone out on the street last night. She had a dog with her."

"Just stop!" he shouted. Joey shook his head. "That girl, Ping . . . She thinks she knows what she's talking about because we live next door to each other. She keeps telling everyone how much of a freak I am."

"That's not how she put it."

"She thinks she's helping, but she's not."

"Ping is nice." It was a lame thing to say, Cassidy knew. She'd only just met her. Besides, this wasn't about Ping.

"For the past year, all the adults have been telling me: There's no such thing as ghosts. Especially not ghost *dogs*. It's all in your head." He stood up, crossed his arms, and slammed his back into the bathroom door. "Don't say a word about Lucky to my mom, or she'll sign you up to talk to a doctor about it too." The door swung open behind him, and he slipped inside.

There was no way she was following him in there. Especially not after *this* conversation.

Cassidy thought of her notebook and the bad things it contained. Maybe later she'd tell Joey about it. Maybe she'd share her secret about the night she'd met her neighbor, Levi Stanton, so Joey would truly understand. Then, maybe he could make a notebook for himself.

"Hey," a voice called from the other end of the hall. Cassidy turned to find Vic peering out from the door to the stairwell. His mouth was puckered tight with what might be annoyance or concern. "I fixed the still life, but we could really use your bag again. You two coming back to class?"

Cassidy's entire body burned with embarrassment. Still, she shook her head. "I'm really sorry about that, really, but we just . . . can't," she said, loud enough for Joey to hear her through the door. "Not today."

CHAPTER FOURTEEN

OF COURSE, Vic called Rose on her cell phone. She was there in moments. She barely glanced at Cassidy as she ushered Joey out of the boys' room, apologizing to Vic several times before the three of them made it out the art center door.

"Well, that was disappointing," she said to Joey. "You maybe want to explain yourself?"

"I just didn't want to be there anymore." Joey climbed into the front seat of the hatchback.

"Did you think about what Cassidy wanted?" Rose asked, her voice trembling as she sat behind the wheel. "You know, not everything is about you, *young man*."

If Cassidy could have folded herself into an envelope, she'd have tucked herself deep inside her backpack. Instead, she slunk down in the seat, trying to make herself invisible. What if Joey revealed that Cassidy had ruined the still life? Or what if he changed his mind and mentioned what she'd said about Lucky, about what she'd seen last night? Rose would be even more furious. This time with her. "I think you owe her an apology."

"It's okay, Rose. I don't mind."

"Nonsense. Joey?"

Joey buckled his safety belt with a fury that could have killed a small animal. "*Sorry*," he said loudly as if to no one. To Cassidy's relief, that was all he said.

Traveling back through the center of Whitechapel, they passed the town hall and the bridges under which the waters merged. Rose pulled into the public parking lot next to the small general store with blue-striped awnings and a sign painted directly onto the window — MORIARTY'S. "I'll pick up some sandwiches for lunch," said Rose. "I've got nothing at home."

As Cassidy followed Rose and Joey into the store, she was met with a cool blast of salty air — pickle brine and potato salad. She'd always loved coming here, though now, it was fraught with Joey's anger. The floors were wide planks and the ceiling was elaborate pressed-tin. Several shelves near the front windows were filled with glass jars containing colorful bulk candy: jawbreakers and taffy and Lemonheads and Fireballs. Beside these was a spinning rack filled with old paperback books and a sign perched on top that read BOOK EXCHANGE: TAKE A COPY, LEAVE A COPY. She turned the frame, looking for one of Levi Stanton's old paperbacks, but there were mostly just Mary Higgins Clarks and James Pattersons and Nathaniel Olmsteads.

The place made her think of olden days, of stories she'd read in school by Laura Ingalls Wilder, people living out on the fron-tier. Joey disappeared into the maze of shelving that was filled with dry goods and other groceries.

Cassidy found Rose in back near the deli counter, by a couple of noisy refrigerators and a generous seating area. Half a dozen people Cassidy recognized from around town — the library, the ice cream parlor, a few other local shops — lounged here on their lunch hours, munching on chips, sipping iced teas and lemonades, chatting quietly to one another. Cassidy thought she recognized a couple who'd been out at Chase Estates yesterday observing the cleanup at the Chambers house.

Behind the counter, an elderly woman was busy wiping down the surfaces of her workstation with a wet cloth. She was plump, dressed in an old-fashioned waitress uniform and hairnet. Her eyebrows appeared to be crooked, and she wore what looked like an excessive amount of blush, a rosy pink. When she saw Rose approach, her face lit up. "Hello, Mrs. Moriarty," Rose chirped, all of her previous fury whisked behind a mask of neighborliness. "Hot enough out there for ya?"

"But I'm not out there, honey," said Mrs. Moriarty. "I'm stuck in here. What can I get for you folks today?"

Rose ordered a couple of Italian submarine sandwiches and half a pound of macaroni salad. Mrs. Moriarty pulled ingredients from the cooler and chatted with Rose over her shoulder. "Quite a to-do out by your place this week. Who knew that Chambers woman was such an old drama queen?" Rose laughed, high-pitched and unnatural, nodding as if they were talking about something other than death.

Cassidy thought of last summer, of the face she'd seen at the Chambers house window, of the woman screaming at her to get off the property. "Drama queen" wasn't the right expression. Yes, Ursula had been cranky — even mean — but she'd obviously been sick. The more Cassidy heard the people of Whitechapel talk about Ursula, the crueler they seemed.

She strolled past every aisle, casually and cautiously looking for Joey. She hadn't meant to stir things up back at the college. She didn't know what her next step should be. After everything she'd been through in the past few years, she wasn't ready to give up on her friendship with him. But had he given up on her? She stepped around the last corner and found him standing several feet away, staring at pet supplies, doggie treats and toys and grooming products. She immediately drew back so he couldn't see her. Cassidy knew he was hurting. She also knew pain faded if you let it. The problem was that strange things were happening, reminders of the past popping up like ghosts — maybe even literally — and poking sharp fingers into his open wound.

Cassidy considered that if she *had* seen Lucky's ghost — an undead, growling version of the once jovial and galumphing mastiff — maybe she and Joey had bigger problems than their dis-integrating friendship.

Voices were raised at the deli counter, and Cassidy turned to see what was wrong. A couple customers who'd been eating their lunch were suddenly involved in an excited exchange with Mrs. Moriarty. She heard the name Ursula and understood what it was all about. One of the elderly men spoke up, nodding, "Stories are spreading all over town. My own grandson called this morning. Says the old coot visited him last night."

Rose stepped away from the counter, her eyes wide. She glanced around, as if looking for Joey, as if she did not want him to hear such things. Cassidy edged up beside her.

"Well I saw her too," said Mrs. Moriarty. The store went silent, all eyes on the deli counter. She smiled as if on stage. "Clear as day, I saw her. Well . . . as clear as day in the middle of the night."

"You *saw* Ursula Chambers," Cassidy repeated.

Reminders of the past popping up like ghosts.

"In my living room." Mrs. Moriarty motioned with her index finger across her heart. "Around eight o'clock. Swear on my hus-band's grave."

Literally.

Cassidy immediately stepped closer, a dull pain jabbing her ribcage. Rose took her hand. "Wow, look at the time," she said, quietly. "Our sandwiches —"

"Now, I'm not proud to admit this next part." Mrs. Moriarty put both hands on the counter and leaned forward. "But my son-in-law told me that the mirror was perfectly fine and that if he hadn't taken it from the pile in front of her house, they would have simply tossed it out with the rest of her garbage." She shook her head, imagining the atrocity. "It's a lovely thing, gorgeous actually. Old wood, perfect little roses carved into the corners. Owen said there'd be *treasure* in those Dumpsters, and he was right. Yesterday, after he left my house, I placed Ursula's mirror on top of my bedroom dresser. It matches perfectly.

"Anyway, I'd been watching my game shows and falling asleep in my chair when I heard a noise behind me. I turned and that's when I saw her. Ursula was standing in my bedroom doorway."

"You must have been dreaming," Rose said, clutching her arms across her chest.

"Maybe I was," said Mrs. Moriarty. "Somehow, I knew why she'd come. Ursula wanted me to bring that mirror back to her house. I think I heard her voice in my head. But she was threatening me. No doubt about it."

"That is creepy!" said a woman sitting at one of the deli tables. "What are you going to do?"

Mrs. Moriarty returned to the open submarine roll and slathered it with mayonnaise. "I don't know." She smiled, as if her story were merely a joke now, an anecdote she'd tell for years. "I guess I'll see if she comes again tonight. If she really wants her mirror back that badly, she can take it herself. I certainly don't have the time to go traipsing through a garbage heap to appease some dead nut job."

Cassidy flinched at the word. Then goose bumps poked up along the back of her neck. She felt a presence and turned to see Joey standing only a few feet away.

When Rose caught Joey's eye, her expression went limp.

He pressed his lips together. Cassidy read his thoughts: *It's okay for you to talk about ghosts, but when I do it . . .*

His mother stepped toward him, reaching for his hand, but Joey had already backed into one of the aisles, making his way to the exit.

In the car, on the way home, Rose turned up the radio and bounced in her seat, as if on the verge of forcing rainbows to stream from her ears. Cassidy knew what she was doing: trying to make them forget everything they'd just heard. Turning into their neighborhood, she shouted over the thrumming beat of an obnoxious pop song, "What say you we close the windows, turn up the AC, and watch some videos this afternoon? Sound like fun?"

To Cassidy's surprise, Joey nodded yes.

MILLIE & THE MIRROR

"THE MAN DOES NOT AGE," Millie said to herself, sitting in the cushy blue reclining chair in the corner of her living room. The man she spoke of was the host of a game show, the one with the wheel that glimmered and spun on her television screen. "If only I were so lucky!" She chuckled, then glanced at the purple rocker on the other side of the room where, once, her husband and the love of her life would have heard her declaration and nodded in agreement. *Too true, Millie*, Georgie Moriarty would have responded. Of course, he'd have also told her that she was beautiful just as she was.

For decades, Mildred Moriarty had been known to her customers as Mrs. Moriarty, but to lovely old Georgie, she'd always been Millie. If she closed her eyes and concentrated, she'd hear his voice calling her: *Silly Millie with the snapdragon smile.*

She sighed as the game show cut to a commercial and plucked the remote from the cushion next to her bottom. She hit the mute button. In the sudden silence, the confusion of the previous night came flooding back to her, when the voice of Ursula the Hermit had whooshed from the darkness behind her. *Bring back my mirror!* Millie had heard Ursula say, possibly only in her head, like words from the final confrontation with a fairy-tale witch.

Millie had leapt from her chair, backing away from the apparition as it faded into the shadows of her bedroom doorway. Later, after brushing her teeth, she'd managed to convince herself that she'd dreamed the vision, that she felt guilty about accepting the odd gift from Owen Chase, her daughter's rich husband. And that was the only way she managed to find sleep that night.

Now, staring at her late husband's rocker, she wished that she *were* being haunted, only not by a loony who'd lived up in the hills, but by the man who'd promised on her wedding day to love, honor, and cherish her until death did they part. *Well*, Millie frowned, *I made a mistake with that one, the segment about parting at death.* Georgie wouldn't have been a scary ghost. He'd be friendly. Like a good memory. She missed him so much. Every day.

Kitty and Owen helped out at the store as much as they could manage, but they had jobs of their own. Kitty had suggested several times recently that Millie should sell the store to Owen, that he'd find some new lucrative use for the space, but Millie could not bear to part with the business she'd created with Georgie almost forty years ago. "Besides," she had explained to Kitty and Owen's dismay, "what would I do with myself all day long? Stare at the wall?"

The show returned with a flurry of flashing lights, and Millie pressed the mute button once more. The theme music filled the room. For years, she'd been playing along with the contestants. She was good at it too, occasionally winning that impossible final round. Once, George had suggested she try out for the show, but she knew she'd never hold up under the pressure. It was all luck, in the end. Pure luck. You could spin the wheel once and lose everything. No. She'd never survive something like that. Better to sit here and play on her own.

Something clattered to the floor, somewhere behind her. It sounded as though it had come from the bedroom. Millie muted the television once again. Trembling, she spun the recliner to face the opposite direction. Her bedroom door stood open, the darkness inside gazing back.

"Who's there?" she called out, forcing anger into her voice, though what she felt, not even very deep down, was fear. Was this really happening again?

In the darkness of her bedroom, something shifted. Moved. It sounded like fabric against fabric. Skin against skin.

Millie choked down the bile that had come up in the back of her throat. She pressed her legs down until the chair's footrest was nestled underneath the cushion, then she stood. "Owen? Is that you? Kitty?"

She knew it was not.

The previous evening, she'd been dozing off. But not now. And after hearing the stories from some of the customers during today's lunch rush, she'd begun to doubt that what she'd seen had been pure imagination. Other folks had seen Ursula as well. And in every instance, they claimed she'd been upset that someone had stolen her belongings. This had to be more than a coincidence.

Unless they'd all had the same dream. . . . Hadn't there been an episode of some old television show in which that had happened — *The X-Files* or something — based on some sort of psychological phenomenon?

A humming began. A low voice, not quite singing, echoed out from the bedroom. Millie nearly fell backward into the recliner.

"That's enough," she said, steadying herself. She stomped loudly across the hardwood floor, to show whoever or whatever was hiding in the darkness that she could be a formidable presence herself. She reached around the edge of the doorway, half expecting a cold finger to brush against her own, then flipped on the overhead light.

Millie braced herself for whatever might be standing there. She gasped when she found the room completely empty. Her floral comforter lay perfectly across the mattress, her pillows still puffy, fluffed by her own hand that very morning.

"Hello?" Millie said, this time unable to control the flutter in her throat. "Ursula?" she whispered, feeling foolish for even considering the possibility. "Is that you?" But there was no answer.

The humming had stopped too. Millie clutched at the fabric of her nightgown near her chest and stepped farther into the room.

The mirror sat on her bureau, facing the bed. Since its surface was perpendicular to her view, Millie could see only a slight reflection of the wood-paneled wall beside it. *The mirror*, thought Millie, wondering suddenly how she could have allowed such a thing into her home. Who knew what kind of filth it had laid in all those years? Who knew what horrors it had witnessed in that disgusting farmhouse? Repulsed, Millie inched closer. Yes, its details were masterfully crafted. But its history . . . its owner.

"You want it?" Millie called out as if Ursula were hiding in the closet, listening to her move across the creaky flooring. "Take it! I didn't ask for it anyhow."

She came around the front of her bureau in full view of the mirror. Its frame was a dark wood, walnut maybe, a couple feet wide by three feet high. She'd propped it against the wall, and now stood staring at herself. Her face was backlit by the overhead light. She rarely flipped that switch. The glare was so harsh, it made her look ancient — had done so even before Millie had thought of herself that way. She turned around to flick on the bedside lamp, when the above light flickered and dimmed.

The floor shuddered slightly and the sound from the television came back on, as if someone had hit the mute button again. A car dealership proclaimed news for *the SALE of the YEAR!* Millie yelped. The room tilted and she reached out for the lip of the bureau to steady herself. The mirror shifted, and the bottom began to slide forward.

Mindlessly, Millie reached out to try to save it, but when she grabbed it, a sharp pain ran across her thumb. She gasped, releasing her grip. The frame bumped against the bureau, jolting her senses. Millie glanced at her thumb. A fresh red line bisected the tip of it. A cut . . . A bite. "Darn it all," she whispered, sticking her thumb in her mouth. A coppery taste rushed over her tongue. She'd need a Band-Aid, if not a stitch or two.

The humming returned. Faintly. Or was it only in her head? The light dimmed further. Millie froze, staring at the mirror. A thin crack had formed at its side. Had it been there before? Was that what she'd cut herself on? It had happened so quickly, Millie wasn't sure.

When Owen and Kitty came over in the morning, she'd tell them to take this thing out of here. Ghosts or not, looking into the mirror chilled her. She pulled her thumb out of her mouth and stepped back, ready to go off in search of that bandage, when she noticed something in the glass behind her. A smudge of darkness. It looked momentarily like a face.

Millie fell forward into the dresser, then turned, expecting to find Ursula there, hands raised to take back what had belonged to her. But there was nothing there. Only the bed, the lamp, the table by the opposite window. The dim light fixture in the ceiling above. Millie shook her head. Someone had been there. Standing behind her. Humming.

Slowly, she glanced back at the mirror. In the glass, the darkness remained, a spherical shape hovering several feet over her mattress. She peered from mirror to bed several times, but the shadowy form only appeared in the reflective glass. For a moment, Millie wondered if she'd dirtied it somehow when she'd sliced her finger.

Leaning forward, she examined the glass. The darkness was no smudge. It was moving, shifting, as if made up of many smaller parts, threads, lacing and intertwining upon itself. She clutched the edge of the bureau, struggling to breathe. A tremor shook the house again, the light of the bedroom dimming even more. She could barely see her own face in the mirror now. The darkness seemed to expand, tendrils of shadow reaching toward her, as if through the surface of the mirror itself. She felt ice on the thin skin of her neck, a slender black chain snaking around her throat like a noose.

From the other room, the game show host was making pronouncements about the final round, but Millie couldn't make out what he said. She didn't care. She couldn't move. She couldn't breathe. Tears spilled from her burning eyes. She tried to call out to her husband — GEORGE! — but nothing escaped the tightness in her throat. All she could see now was darkness. All she could feel was cold. A tingling in her fingertips. A sense of weightlessness, as if she were falling in slow motion.

"Oh, I'm sorry," the host's voice blared moments later from the television, sounding purposely crestfallen. "Let's see what you could have won." The audience gasped in disappointment.

CHAPTER FIFTEEN

IT HAD BEEN A SLOW MORNING, nothing like the one before. Dennis, Deb, and Rose had all left early for work and various errands. Cassidy figured that she and Joey had run Rose through an emotional rinse cycle, and if she had anything else planned for their summer, it would most likely come much later. Now, it was only the two of them left to clean up in silence after breakfast.

Despite the calm end to the previous day, Joey had finished the evening withdrawn, stuck in his head, ignoring Cassidy almost entirely. Before retiring to her room upstairs, she had caught sight of Ping in the driveway next door with her two brothers and went out to say hello.

She'd been happy to share her strange day with Ping. When she mentioned the figures she'd seen out in the street the previous night, Ping looked curious but unsurprised. This was a *strange state* they were living in after all. Cassidy went on about the conversation she'd tried to have with Joey during the art class, then about the visit to the general store, where she'd heard that people had been seeing the ghost of Ursula Chambers. They'd agreed to get together the next day, with Joey or without.

Outside, the air was misty, the sky covered in thick clouds. Deb had left the Weather Channel blaring from the television in the living room, and once Cassidy had finished loading the dishwasher, she plopped down on the sofa and switched the channel to the Cartoon Network. To her surprise, Joey eventually came over and perched on the other side of the couch. They sat together just like that through a few old episodes of *Adventure Time*, though several times, Cassidy just stopped herself from leaning over and asking him what he thought about the ghost stories they'd overheard yesterday at Moriarty's. She was dying to know if he'd woken sporadically in the night like she had, heart pounding, limbs tingling, ears straining to hear shuffling sounds out on the street, but she didn't want a repeat performance of his art class explosion.

There was a knock at the sliding door. A dark shadow stood outside on the patio, holding up hands to peer through the glass. Joey groaned, but got up to answer it. He slid open the door and asked, "What the heck do *you* want?"

Cassidy sighed. She had hoped he was done taking that tone.

"Is Cassidy here?" It was Ping.

Joey nodded toward the living room. Cassidy sat up straight and waved. "Hi!" Ping slipped past Joey and into the kitchen.

"Sure! Come on in!" Joey said, waving his arms to indicate that he was not in fact invisible.

"Thank you." Ping nodded politely. Cassidy couldn't tell if she was oblivious to his sarcasm or if she was merely awesome. Ping winked, and Cassidy stifled laughter. "Hey, did you guys see the news this morning?"

"Of course," said Joey. "We never miss the stock report. It's so fascinating."

Ping ignored him, stepping closer to Cassidy. "You'll both want to know," she whispered, eyeing Joey briefly. He scowled and slammed the sliding door before stomping back to his spot on the couch.

"Forget it," said Ping, holding up a hand. "Cassidy, let's take a walk."

"Wait," said Joey, looking suddenly frightened to be left alone. He took a deep breath. "Is it about Ursula?"

Ping raised an eyebrow, then nodded. "You sure you want to hear about it?"

He closed his eyes, mouthing the word *yes*.

"Okay then. They lost her."

"They what?" Cassidy said at the same time Joey asked, "They, *who*?"

"The funeral parlor over in . . . I forget where. But a couple days ago, the day of the burial in fact, the morticians opened the casket and found it empty. I heard about it this morning on the *Today* show. One of those *weird* stories."

"Someone *stole* Ursula Chambers?" Joey was pale, his lips open slightly, trying to keep his breath even.

"That's their theory."

"And what's your theory? That she just got up and walked away?"

Ping turned pink. No one spoke. Joey glanced between the two girls, then leapt up and ran toward the stairs.

CHAPTER SIXTEEN

THE CURTAINS WERE STILL DRAWN in Joey's bedroom, so when Cassidy and Ping climbed the stairs behind him, they walked in darkness. From the hall, they heard him rummaging around. A blipping sound rang out, and the blue light of a computer screen spilled into the hallway.

"Are you okay?" Cassidy dared to call through his open door.

"Yeah," he said. "I just want to see if I can find something about this on my computer." After a moment, he added, "It's really weird with you guys standing there watching me."

Cassidy sighed, then wandered into the room, stepping over piles of clothes that lay like booby traps across the floor. She pulled open the curtains and grayish light filtered into the small space. Ping stood behind Joey at his desk.

It took him a couple minutes, but eventually he found the page he was looking for. "Here we go," he said, pulling out his desk chair and sitting down. *"Hoarder Mystery Deepens as Corpse Disappears,"* he read. The story went just as Ping had told it.

"She's just *gone*," said Ping.

Joey turned to look at the girls. "Like Lucky," he whispered. "You do believe me now. Don't you?"

"I believed you *before*," said Cassidy. "That's what I was trying to tell you yesterday, when you" — *totally FREAKED OUT* — "you know, left the art class."

"I've seen him too," Ping added. "Your dog. Out by the oak tree in your backyard."

Joey turned his chair around. Quietly, carefully, he said, "I thought you were making fun of me."

"Well, there's nothing fun about this," said Ping with a wry grin, as if this was the exact kind of thing she found to be if not fun then at least intriguing.

"Downstairs," said Cassidy, "Ping mentioned that the theft was only one theory of what happened to the body. But what's the other theory? Is there a connection between Joey's missing dog and our missing hermit?"

"Besides you seeing them walk down the street the other night?" Ping asked, wide-eyed.

Cassidy's skin tingled. "But that's not what I saw," she insisted.

"It's not?" Ping squeaked out. "You sure?"

"The walking dead," said Cassidy, her memory wandering into the shadow world of Monday night. "It's not possible."

"But it happened."

Joey swallowed violently, as if choking down some sick. "You guys are *really* thinking that this stuff is real? You're not joking?"

"We're not joking," said Ping. "Why do you keep asking that?"

"It's just that . . . for the past year, whenever I've told anyone what I've seen or heard, they laughed at me. And then, with my parents sending me to talk to Dr. Caleb . . . It's all just been . . . confusing."

As Cassidy listened to Joey talk, she thought of the Joey she used to know. The boy who spoke softly, kindly, who'd have done anything to make her summer the best summer it could be. Feeling something in her own chest open up, she fell back onto his bed and clutched at his sheets, as if that could stop her from melting into a tearful mess.

"*Confusing* isn't quite the right word," said Ping.

"Close enough," said Joey, turning back to his computer screen.

Cassidy waited for the pressure behind her eyes to dissipate before going on. "So, let's say there is a connection between what I've seen over the past few days and the missing body." She glanced at the back of Joey's head and added, "Bodies."

"Could it have to do with what you guys overheard yesterday at the deli?" asked Ping.

Joey turned around, mouth agape. He shook his head at Cassidy. "Word travels fast around here."

"We chatted last night," said Ping. "Cassidy caught me up on what happened."

"The *connection*," said Cassidy. "According to the stories we heard at Moriarty's, people all over Whitechapel have seen her. Ursula."

"Yeah," said Ping, "but not just *anyone*. You said that Ursula has appeared to those who took something from the Dumpsters in her driveway. She'd warned them to bring her stuff back. Or else. Does this confirm that Ursula's visitations aren't just hallucinations?"

"Possibly," said Cassidy.

Ping began, "So if this supernatural stuff is plausible —"

"It *is*," Joey added.

"Then the question is, have these people in Whitechapel been seeing Ursula's ghost? Or have they seen Ursula herself?"

CHAPTER SEVENTEEN

AN ENGINE RUMBLED into the driveway. From Joey's bedroom window, Cassidy watched Rose climb out of the white hatchback, grappling with several bags of groceries. "Your mom's home," she said to Joey. The three peered out the window. "Looks like she needs help."

"We can continue this later," said Ping.

They all made their way downstairs. Outside, the spitting mist coated their faces as they made their way to the car. When Rose saw them approaching, her eyes lit up. "Oh, wow. Volunteers," she said with a smile. "Hi there, Ping. Nice to see you." Ping nodded hello.

As Cassidy took a couple of heavy paper bags from Rose, she sensed that something was wrong. Rose's skin was practically green and her long neck was slouched as if she were wearing a heavy coat instead of a light pink tank top. By the time they'd emptied the car and brought all of the groceries to the kitchen, Joey'd noticed too. "You okay, Mom?"

Rose dropped a head of lettuce into the vegetable drawer in the fridge. She straightened her spine and twisted her neck slightly, releasing a disturbing cracking noise. After a moment, she said, almost to herself, "I suppose you're going to hear about it eventually." The three kids sat on the high stools at the countertop that divided the kitchen from the living room. Rose closed the refrigerator door, then leaned against it. "I've got some bad news."

❖

Mrs. Moriarty was dead.

Cassidy stopped listening after she'd heard those words, her mind racing through what she remembered of yesterday, of the old woman's ghostly tale from behind the deli counter. Something about a mirror that had belonged to Ursula. A gift from her son-in-law. She remembered Mr. Chase from the day she'd arrived back in Whitechapel — the man who'd been fascinated with Ursula's taxidermy animals. Foxes.

Rose was still talking — *asphyxiation, choking, possible stroke, they discovered the body this morning* — but Cassidy could think only of Ursula's threat.

"Cassidy?" Rose said. "Are you feeling okay?"

Cassidy lifted her forehead from the countertop, not realizing that she'd even lowered it. "It's just . . . we saw Mrs. Moriarty *yesterday.*" She glanced at Ping and Joey who were wide-eyed, their faces empty of blood. She knew they were piecing together everything they'd been talking about upstairs only minutes earlier.

Could it be that these were merely coincidences? Ursula's ghostly appearance followed by the passing of Mrs. Moriarty? The discovery of the missing corpse right after Cassidy's nightmare vision two nights prior?

When no one else responded, Rose flushed, realizing that she'd opened a can of snakes that would be difficult now to contain. "These things happen," she said. "It's sad, of course, but Mrs. Moriarty lived a long, good life. And now she's with her husband."

Cassidy wanted to speak up, to tell Rose about Ping's and Joey's theories on the subject, but she remembered what Joey had said he'd been through in the year since Lucky's death. Rose wouldn't hear her. In fact, she might even get angry and send her back to the city. Only yesterday that idea might have seemed like a good thing. Now, however, she felt like Joey, and in a way even Ping, needed her here.

Rose clapped her hands. "Okay then!" she shouted. "No more gloom and doom! Let's make some lunch and then we're off. I don't know where to but it'll be someplace fun. Ping, call your mom and tell her. We're going on an adventure."

Despite the widening pit Cassidy felt in her stomach, she remembered once more why she'd loved coming to Whitechapel, even if, this time around, it had become a twisted version of the past.

CHAPTER EIGHTEEN

ROSE AND THE THREE KIDS piled into the car. Several miles north of Chase Estates, hidden amidst several bends of the road, was a thrift store called Graceland Refurbishments. Locals referred to it as Junkland.

Cassidy remembered visiting the store her first year in Whitechapel, astounded by the rows of old furniture stacked on top of one another, how they formed a makeshift labyrinth that was easy to get lost in. Junkland was an appealing destination for families, especially on rainy days, because its contents were so diverse, almost like a curio museum. There were antique toys, rare and used books, old postcards that contained snippets of lives written on their backs, posters, paintings, magazines — knickknacks of all sorts — arranged in a surprisingly organized fashion.

By the time Rose had pulled into the dirt lot, Cassidy had grown anxious for a diversion from her own dark thoughts. No one had said much during the ride, and she knew that they were all ruminating on the pieces of strange news that had come to them that morning. So, when Rose shoved the car's gear into park, the small group burst from the doors and raced toward the store's entrance as if toward an empty line for a roller coaster at Six Flags.

Inside the main entrance, Rose handed them each two dollars, challenging them to locate the most interesting piece of "junk" in the store. The winner, judged by Rose, would get an extra ten bucks to spend. "Let's meet back here in, say, twenty minutes."

Junkland had a sweet aroma, a mix of old wood and fruity cleaning product. It would have been a little nauseating if it had been stronger, but as Cassidy followed Ping and Joey deeper into the cavernous space, she grew used to it until eventually, it disappeared. Rose's contest was in the back of their minds as they settled into a secluded corner piled with old books and magazines.

"So what do we do now?" Cassidy asked.

"What *can* we do?" Joey replied. "Adults never listen to what I say."

Cassidy tried, "But if the three of us mention it together —"

"They'll think I roped you into this," Joey interrupted.

Ping shook her head. "If Ursula Chambers, or her ghost, or *something*, is really going around killing people who stole from her, then Whitechapel's gonna be in real trouble, real soon."

Cassidy thought of her book, of its power to diminish her fears, of the strength it had returned to her over the past few years. "This could all still be coincidence. Right?" she said. Joey and Ping glanced at each other, but said nothing. "So then let's just forget about it as best we can. Let's play Rose's game. Try to have fun for a while. Okay?"

The three split up, scouring the store for the most interesting two-dollar item they could find. Cassidy came upon one aisle of glass cases displaying small crystalline figurines: animals, circus performers, ballerinas. One of these figures caught her eye, a tiny pink elephant, its delicate trunk uplifted as if to trumpet. Cassidy bent down to check out the sticker stuck on its underside — $1.99. Perfect! When she slid the case open, she noticed that its two tusks had been chipped, the tips nicked off. Even with the elephant's obvious damage, Cassidy's heart raced as she headed back toward the store's entrance for the rendezvous, hoping that Rose would choose her as the winner.

She came around a corner and found the trio. Rose waved. Joey and Ping each held an item of their own behind their backs. "You ready?" Rose asked as Cassidy approached.

"I hope so," she said, the glass elephant enclosed in her fist, poking at her palm.

They went around in a circle. Ping revealed four old copies of her favorite magazine, *Strange State*. Rose shook her head, in awe of the quantity, if not exactly the quality, of Ping's choice. Cassidy went next. When she opened her hand, the group all oohed and aahed — even Joey — and Cassidy knew that her little discovery was special. "Nice," said Rose. Joey was last. From behind his back, he removed a large yellowed piece of paper rolled up tight. Rose helped him stretch out the scroll. It was an old map.

Looking closer, Cassidy recognized the names of several roads and streams. The map depicted a version of Whitechapel from many years ago. None of the recent housing developments existed yet. Everything looked like it must have been so pristine. Untouched. Pure. She had to admit, it was a pretty cool artifact, but would it trump her pink elephant?

"Uh-oh," said Rose, glancing at the back of the map. "You've got one big problem here, buddy. It's priced at $2.25. Over the limit."

"But I figured I could bargain it down."

Rose peered at Cassidy and Ping. "Do you girls think that's fair?"

"NO!" they both shouted, then laughed. For a moment, Cassidy was flushed with guilt, but then Joey smirked and rolled his eyes and threw his hands into the air.

Rose nodded sagely. "Then I must say that the trophy goes to . . ." She paused dramatically. "Cassidy Bean!"

Cassidy emitted a high-pitched squeal. A few other customers stared at her. She didn't care — the embarrassment was worth the prize. She closed the figurine in her fist once more, and after Rose handed over the tenner, Cassidy strolled back to the aisle of glass cases to pick out a couple companions for her elephant, whom she'd already decided to name Triumphant.

By the time the group was back in the car, they were consumed by their new treasures. On the ride home, they rolled out Joey's map, which he had bargained down to two dollars, across their laps, pointing out missing landmarks, forgotten roads, dried up rivers, and more, as they traveled through their changed version of the world that had once existed on that old yellowed paper.

CASSIDY'S BOOK OF BAD THINGS, ENTRY #20:
GETTING LOST

Today at school, Mr. Faros told us stories from Greek mythology. He mentioned a whole bunch of stuff about Kings and their sons and gods and goddesses and revenge.

What stuck out most for me was the story of the Minotaur's labyrinth on Crete. According to the myth, every few years, this King named Minos forced a group of Kids to go into this giant maze on his island, where a monster called the Minotaur, who was a giant man with a bull's head, waited to chomp their bones.

I Know. Disgusting.

Eventually, there was this one guy, his name was Theseus, who came along and volunteered to enter the labyrinth and hunt down the beast. And I thought, WHO WOULD DO THAT? What Kind of person would volunteer for certain death? He'd have to be crazy. Well, I guess sometimes crazy wins, because Theseus ended up slaying the Minotaur and becoming a hero.

Mr. Faros told us to think of the tale like a metaphor. Like: What does the labyrinth represent? Dreams? Fears? Death? But, I thought, what if it doesn't represent anything? What if it was just a place where horrible things happened?

Anyway, for the rest of the day, I haven't been able to stop imagining this labyrinth — the stone maze that someone built so they could torture hordes of young people. Did something like that actually exist? And could it exist again today?

Once, on a field trip to the Metropolitan Museum of Art, I got separated from my group. I guess I'd been staring too long at one of the intricately painted Egyptian coffins. I wandered around for what felt like forever, falling deeper and deeper into the depths of the building, looking for Mrs. Flannigan and my class, but they'd disappeared. All these thoughts ran through my head. What if someone kidnapped all of them? What if the museum somehow ate them? What if they were all playing a joke on me, and once we were back at school, everyone would point and laugh and say what an idiot I was? I knew I could find my way back to Brooklyn if I had to, but deep down I was filled with dread that I'd never see anyone I knew ever again.

Eventually, a security guard made an announcement over the intercom, asking me to approach one of the museum staff, which I did. They brought me back to the lobby where I found Mrs. Flannigan waiting for me with tears in her eyes. She hugged me until I couldn't breathe. And I cried too, finally realizing how terrified I'd been.

Tonight, I've been imagining myself inside the Minotaur's maze. In the dark. Turning left. Turning right. Not knowing where I'm going. And around every corner, there could be this giant thing reaching out for me, waiting there to snatch me and stick me in its mouth and chew me up and swallow me down.

CHAPTER NINETEEN

NO ONE SAID A WORD when, pulling into the Tremonts' driveway, they saw two large trucks pass in the opposite direction, heading away from the cul-de-sac, carting off the Dumpsters that had been parked in Ursula's overgrown driveway since the beginning of the week.

Climbing out of the hatchback's backseat, Cassidy felt nauseated thinking about all of Ursula's junk disappearing into a landfill somewhere — it was the opposite of what the old woman must have wished. She stood at the end of the driveway with Ping, watching as the trucks rumbled off around the corner, the sound of their engines echoing through the valley. Both girls sighed, then dashed toward the Tremonts' porch as the rain really started to come down.

Stepping into the foyer, Cassidy overheard Rose speaking quietly to Joey. Something that sounded like *thank you*. And *I'm proud of you*. She didn't hear Joey's answer but knew enough to steer Ping toward the living room, where they squatted on the floor beside the coffee table to examine the treasures that Rose had been kind enough to buy them at Junkland.

Cassidy used her T-shirt to buff Triumphant, as well as the small porcelain penguin and the tiny plastic pig on which she'd used her reward money. Ping flipped through the magazines, her long dark hair obscuring both her face and the articles that caught her attention.

Eventually, Joey wandered over carrying his map of Whitechapel. He knelt beside them, silently spreading open the map so that it covered most of the coffee table. Cassidy helped him weigh down the curled edges of paper, placing the remote control on one corner and her new tiny pets on another. Ping placed several copies of *Strange State* on the corner closest to her, and Joey used a PlayStation controller to secure the last.

Cassidy glanced over the map, remembering what Joey had pointed out on the ride home, the old trails that were no longer there, the streets that had appeared where once only cornfields had grown. She imagined her own neighborhood in Brooklyn, wondering how drastically a map from this same time period, maybe a hundred years ago, would have reflected the change in her everyday landscape. The world back then had been completely different. Fewer trains. Wider streets. Smaller buildings. The skyline of present-day New York belonged to a different city than the one of old.

Picking up where they'd left off in the car, Joey said, "Did you guys notice what was missing when we drove through the entrance into Chase Estates a few minutes ago?" It was a playful question, Cassidy thought, but Joey's eyebrows were set in a serious line, his mouth pulled into a knowing smirk.

"Missing?" Ping asked.

Joey pointed to a section near the center of the map, just off the main road. Cassidy leaned closer and saw what he meant. The road clearly passed a site that had been marked "Chambers Farm." A little rectangle was drawn near the road, labeled "house."

"Oh hey," said Cassidy, trying to sound excited, "that's where we are."

"Not quite," said Joey. "The cul-de-sac should be farther back, away from the road." He slid his finger east about three inches. "Here."

Ping shook her head. "That can't be right. This map says that the Chambers farmhouse should be right next to the main street. But the only thing that's there now —"

"Is the entrance to Chase Estates," Joey finished.

"Weird," said Cassidy. She shuddered, thinking about the abandoned place a few hundred yards up the hillside. Outside, the wind picked up, heaving rain at the house, coating the screens so thickly in water that she could barely see out into the shadowed backyard. "I thought that Ursula lived in the original farmhouse. Your dad told me that when I asked him about it a long time ago. But it's not where this map says it was."

"Nope," said Joey. "Either the house up the hill isn't the original farmhouse . . ." He paused, nodding in the direction of the overgrown driveway. "Or someone moved it."

"Moved it?" Ping said. "How the heck do you *move* a house?"

"I've heard of ways," Joey said. "I think there's a bigger question: *Why* would you move a house?"

OWEN & THE ANIMALS

OWEN CHASE SAT at his computer trying to catch up on work, but he could not concentrate. Death and the storm had kept his mind sequestered for the past hour. The rain showed no sign of letting up. It roared against the skylight in the dim office at the rear of his house — the most impressive house in all of the development.

Chase Estates. Owen had named it after himself. So what if the rest of the town thought him to be an egomaniacal pig? If they'd had the money or the clout, he was certain they'd have done the same. The American Way.

Owen had purchased the land from an elderly farmer named Aidan Chambers almost fifteen years prior, decreeing after breaking ground that no other home raised in this development would ever exceed his own five-thousand-plus square feet of living space. And yet, on nights like this, when the rain flew and the wind bellowed, Owen longed for a cozier space, something with less marble, lower ceilings — something like the home he'd grown up in on Long Island, out past the urban reach of New York City.

Sometimes, he imagined his mother was in the next room, baking her famous chocolate-chip cookie pie as he sat and watched those now classic television shows. *Andy Griffith. Mister Ed. I Love Lucy.* These memories haunted him, especially when he was alone in "the palace," as his wife liked to call their home.

Tonight, however, Owen was not alone. Kitty was upstairs, lying down, having taken something to calm her nerves. She had been torn to pieces when he gave her the news about her mother, Millie, that morning. The rest of the day they'd spent making calls, answering calls, accepting condolences, giving condolences. There'd barely been enough time to consult with the Monsignor and finally with Dalton's Funeral Home down in the center of Whitechapel before the end of business hours. Now, Owen's email inbox was flooded, and he felt as though he'd never catch up.

The sound of the rain and the wind was not helping. Nor was his memory of the previous night, when he'd received a very unwelcome visitor . . .

He wondered if Kitty had an extra of whatever it was she took. Maybe he'd forget about the rest of the work he was trying to catch up on and join her upstairs.

No, he thought after a moment, *if it happens again, I want to be sure my mind is clear. But a beer wouldn't hurt, would it?*

After struggling to rise from the chair's sunken seat, he stumbled, exhausted, toward the office door. Swinging it open, he saw the short dark hallway that led to the cavernous foyer beyond. Thankfully, Kitty had left one set of sconces glowing faintly, so that he might find his way to the bottom of the winding grand staircase.

Flicking off the light in the room behind him, Owen continued toward the glow of the foyer, passing by the garage door on his left where he'd stored most of the stuff he taken from the Hermit's driveway. He paused, his curiosity keeping him still.

Just last night, he'd stood in the same spot, a dull whiskey buzz numbing his limbs, when he'd heard something on the other side of the door. His fuzzy mind quickly provided an image: A couple of the neighborhood delinquents had broken in and were looting his taxidermy trove. Owen had swung the door open with a loud crash. The motion-activated light was already on, and beyond the open garage door a vague indigo dusk obscured his driveway. To his surprise, there were no teenagers rummaging through his belongings; instead, to his horror, he found himself staring into the eyes of Ursula Chambers, who was standing in the direct center of the garage.

She'd been dressed in a silvery purple jogging suit, white stripes running up the sides of her plump legs, her skin sallow, almost gray. As he stared in shock, he noticed streetlights peering back at him through her. He'd clutched at the doorframe to catch himself from fainting. Ursula had turned her head slowly, seeming to take in the scene, the piles of taxidermy animals that had once inhabited her home up on the hill — the fox, the badger, the owl, the hawk — the treasure that Owen had hoped to make a mint from at the Hudson House Auction in the fall.

When Ursula had glanced back in his direction, her eyes flared with anger. She didn't need to say a word for him to understand what she was trying to communicate: Return the items to the house. Or else.

"Get out of here!" Owen had screamed at the thing. "Get out! Get out! Get out!" By the time Kitty had come running, the apparition had gone. In fact, it had dissolved into nothingness even before he'd spit out the final word of his rampage.

Now, all that seemed like it had been a dream. A vivid hallucination. Something he'd seen in a scary movie. Bad things happened all the time — more often than most people were willing to admit — but *ghosts*? Ghosts existed only in the realm of fiction.

He imagined Millie, her eyes crimson, laughing at him with shimmering Ursula, their voices rising and crackling and piercing the night. How funny to watch a grown man shiver at the thought of two dead old ladies. A real hoot it must be.

Now, to reassure himself, Owen reached out, for the second night in a row, to tug open the door to the garage. This time, the room was pitch dark. Sheets of rain waved against the automatic doors. Quickly, he reached inside and flicked on the lights. Bright fluorescents flickered from the ceiling. The space was empty. Owen released a deep sigh. He chuckled to himself, not feeling particularly jolly, mostly foolish. Had he really thought he'd find them there, waiting for him?

He was about to close the door and head upstairs, when he glanced inside one more time. It was then he noticed that the four dead animals that he'd leaned against his tool storage shelves were gone.

For a moment, Owen thought again of intruders, but quickly, his mind moved on to darker possibilities. Early that morning, he'd meant to head back over to the farmhouse with the animals, right after he'd stopped at his mother-in-law's house to drive her to the store. After being so shaken by the sight of Ursula standing in his garage the previous night, he figured that whatever easy cash he could have made from the auction was not worth a summertime of nightmares. But of course, the day had made other plans for Owen. For Millie. For Kitty. And so the animals had remained in his garage.

Except . . . they hadn't. Someone had taken them.

Owen clicked off the fluorescent lights and closed the door, turning back toward the glow of the foyer. "Honey?" he called out as he ambled slowly forward, hoping she might appear at the top landing, arms open, wearing her beauty-queen smile. But his own voice bounced around the house's entryway. *Honey, honey, honey . . .*

If he could have seen himself, could pause to imagine the sight of a six-foot tall, three-hundred pound man tiptoeing breathlessly into the marble foyer, he may have stopped and shook away his fear, doubling over in giddy laughter at his childish behavior, but his mind was keeping pace with his heart, and both had begun to hurt. Just before he crept into the light of the new room, a different sort of sound resonated off the heights of marble and stone. Somewhere in the house a click-clack, click-clack clatter of claws tapped a tile floor.

He froze. Had an animal found its way inside, trying to escape from the storm?

Click-clack. Click-clack. Something was moving through the dining room on the other side of the foyer. Coming closer. If he didn't go immediately, it would find him standing there. The thought terrified him. Silently, he stepped backward, hoping to hide himself in the hallway's shadow.

Growling and screeching sounds swirled resonantly around the space, mixing in awful harmony, like off-pitch voices of the children's choir singing in church on Sundays.

Owen turned and ran. The noise of scrabbling claws erupted behind him. A high-pitched scream followed it, and Owen Chase, barreling toward his office door, released his own desperate howl. He grabbed the knob and swung the door open. He slipped inside, slammed it shut, then turned and leaned against it. He pressed the button in the center of the knob. The lock clicked.

The rain had calmed. The room was dark, his desk a vague silhouette against the far window. Owen felt pressure in his ears, the thudding of his own blood rushing into his head. He clutched his hands to his scalp, stepping silently away from the door. He wondered if this was what going crazy felt like. Or maybe he was in shock from finding Millie dead on the floor. "Kitty!" he called out again and again, shouting until his throat was raw. But then he thought, what if she wakes up? What if she comes downstairs? What if she discovers what was making those noises?

The noises . . . They'd stopped. He pressed his ear against the door, but the house was now quiet. If there *was* something in the hall, he couldn't allow his wife to stumble into it. He had to be sure. He turned the knob; the lock snapped open. He pulled on the door, peering into the dim crack. The hall was empty. Either the sounds had been in his head, or the thing had moved on to another part of the house.

Bang!

Something toppled to the floor behind him. As lightning flashed, Owen spun. Perched on his desk were two shapes. Bright images of the hawk and the badger were etched into Owen's sight. The hawk spread its wings in the darkness. The badger reared up, hissing. Owen raised his arms in defense. The office door creaked open as the other two specimens slipped quietly inside. None of them were quiet for long.

CASSIDY'S BOOK OF BAD THINGS, ENTRY #22:
HAUNTINGS

Mr. Stanton told me that a person can be haunted by a memory of something bad. I guess that's why I started writing in this notebook. My memories.

But most people hear "hauntings," and they think "ghosts."

Some say a person can become a ghost if they have unfinished business leftover from their life. They might never have gotten the chance to tell someone that they love them, so their spirit lingers, eternally hopeless. Or a person might have been murdered, and in death, they long to tell the living who it was that wronged them. Either that, or the ghost might try to take their own vengeance.

At the cemetery near my apartment building, there is lots of strange energy, at least according to Janet and Benji. They say they've heard all sorts of stories about ghosts haunting the grounds. I've always wondered, What kind? The kind that loves? The kind that kills? Or the kind that are only memories?

Once, the three of us went walking there after school. We wandered the twisted paths, up and down hills, snaking past gravestones and monuments. Janet had brought her phone, which has a pretty good camera in it. We came to one spot where a large mausoleum was built into the steep hillside, so that the roof of the weird building actually met the lawn.

Above the door, a name had been carved into the stone. WHITNEY. The entrance had been boarded up. A crooked gate was locked across the boards with rusted chains. Benji was the one who'd noticed that there was space at the bottom of the doorway to see inside. Staring into the darkness, we saw a set of stairs leading down into shadow.

At the bottom of the stairs was a room, and at the back of the room was a wall made up of small compartments. Janet explained that this was where the Whitney family was entombed, that each compartment contained a dead body. I stumbled back, but she leaned forward, pulled her phone from her pocket, and reached through the bars to take a picture.

A weird thing happened when we got back to Janet and Benji's place. She uploaded the pic to her computer, where we could examine it on a bigger screen. What we saw gave us goose bumps on top of our goose bumps. In the middle of the tomb, there was a bluish mist. And in the middle of the mist, Janet pointed out, a pair of black eyes was staring up at us. We could just make out the shape of a head, thrown back. Its mouth was twisted open. Janet deleted the picture immediately, then yanked the computer's plug out of the wall, even though I told her that might mess everything up.

Later, when I was trying to sleep, I thought about ghosts. Then I thought about the cemetery and Janet's picture. I wonder, when I am dead, will my ghost hang around on earth for unfinished business? What business did the figure in the mist have down in the darkness of the tomb? The thing didn't look human. And then I wondered if what Janet had captured on her camera might be something other than a ghost. But what? A ghoul? A demon? Or something worse? Something I can't even imagine?

I never got all the way to sleep that night. And I haven't been back to the cemetery since.

Chapter Twenty

CASSIDY WAS WOKEN the next morning by distant sirens. Normally, in the city, this wouldn't have bothered her — she might even not have heard them — but in Whitechapel, the noise was jarring.

She opened her eyes to the dim light of Tony's curtained bedroom. She slid her hand under her pillow and caught her finger on the hard edge of her notebook. She pulled out the book and glanced down at the page to which she'd opened it the previous night. *Hauntings*.

The rain and the wind had pummeled the valley. Usually, on nights like that, Cassidy would open the book to whatever entry might best help her sort out what was frightening her most. Some people had dream catchers hanging over their beds; Cassidy had her *Book of Bad Things* tucked beneath her pillow.

She closed the book and stuck it in her backpack, then she marched to the window opposite the bed and pulled back the curtain. By then, the sirens had stopped, but in the dawn's glow, she could see flashing lights down the hill, parked in front of a large house near the entrance of the development. Police cars or fire trucks or an ambulance. Cassidy couldn't tell.

She made her way to the bathroom. The sounds of television drifted up from downstairs in the living room. Deb and Dennis must be up, getting ready for their early days. After washing her hands and splashing water on her face, Cassidy galloped down the stairs to see if she could catch them before they left. She'd barely chatted with either of them since early in the week. She found them, father and daughter, sitting together on the front porch, perched on the dew-damp white wicker furniture, drinking from steaming mugs.

"Cassidy!" said Dennis. "We haven't seen nearly enough of you!" Deb raised her mug sleepily.

Cassidy smiled and shrugged. "We still have plenty of time before I head back to the city."

"I hope my son's been treating you all right," said Dennis. "I know he's been a little mopey lately."

Mopey? Cassidy thought. *That's one way to put it.* "We've been having fun."

Dennis glanced at his daughter, then nudged her leg with his knee.

Deb sat up straight. "Speaking of fun," she said, clearing her throat, her eyelids still heavy, "they're showing *Jaws* on the lawn in the center of town tonight. I'm going with my friend Julie, but there's room in the car for a couple more. You and Joey wanna join us?"

Dennis had obviously goaded Deb into making an invitation. Still, Cassidy wasn't going to pass up an outdoor movie in Whitechapel, even if Joey was being *mopey*. "Sure! I hope you don't mind if I cover my eyes."

"Only if you don't mind if I scream my head off," Deb said, laughing. "Dad, you sure you and Mom don't want to come too?" Cassidy blushed, imagining inviting her own mother to go out somewhere. Naomi would have died.

"If I can get home from the city early enough, I'll try my best. My god, that movie . . ." he said, shuddering as he stood. Stepping through the screen door, he added, "But I suppose this town could use a good distraction."

A chill wind rustled the small leaves of the potted plants Rose kept on the porch. The sky was filled with pink clouds, light blue beyond. The storm had blown away the heat and humidity. Maybe the troubles of Whitechapel were gone too?

Deb squinted up the street, toward the top of the cul-de-sac and the overgrown driveway there. "Weird stuff happening lately," she said, as if reading Cassidy's mind. "Makes me wonder if there was something to those stories Joey's been telling for the past year." Glancing at Cassidy, she smirked. "Ghosts and zombies! Ha. You don't believe in that stuff?"

"Not sure," said Cassidy, shrugging, then sitting down on a rocking chair and hugging her arms against the chill. "I believe in what I can see, I guess."

"Then let's hope you don't see Ursula Chambers wandering around Whitechapel," Deb sniffed, nonchalantly. "I hear there's been a lot of that going around."

"You have?"

"Yeah." Deb nodded. "The folks at the greenhouse where I'm interning this summer say they've seen her themselves."

Cassidy glanced up the street, remembering the Dumpsters that had sat there until yesterday. "Did your friends say anything about her house? Did they take anything from her driveway when the crew was cleaning up?"

Deb sipped her coffee, staring into Cassidy's eyes, squinting with concern. "Yeah, as a matter of fact. Also said Ursula showed up in the middle of the night, telling them to put it back." She chuckled. "They're all having some sort of mass hallucination. It would seem so ridiculous to me, except for the fact that Mrs. Moriarty really died."

Cassidy shivered. Was it that cold out here? "You're going to the greenhouse today?"

"Yup. In a few."

"Can you do something for me?"

"Sure. What is it?"

"Tell your friends who've seen Ursula, the ones you work with, to put it back."

"Put what back?"

Cassidy glanced toward the flashing lights that were still parked down the hill. Fingers of ice ran along her spine, and this time she knew it wasn't the breeze. "Tell them to put back whatever they took from her."

CHAPTER TWENTY-ONE

INSIDE, ROSE WAS PUTTERING about in the kitchen. When she saw Cassidy, she cried out, "No more rain!"

"Yay!" said Cassidy softly, waving her hands in halfhearted excitement.

"How about we go get that lazybones out of bed," Rose said, shaking a thumb toward Joey's room at the top of the stairs. "Then we'll hop in the car and take a trip out to Quarry Lake for a morning swim? Heck, maybe we'll make a day of it!"

Cassidy imagined his reaction if she pounded on his door. "Can we invite Ping too?" she asked.

Quarry Lake was up in the hills off the main road, several miles past Junkland. As its name suggested, the lake had once been the site of an old rock quarry, but sometime in the past fifty or so years, had been turned into a swimming hole. A field of grass, shaded intermittently by a few mature oaks, led to the water's edge. On the far side of the lake, a sheer cliff rose about thirty feet from the surface. At the top of this rock wall, thick woods — pine and scrub — seemed poised to leap past the periphery and into the deep water below.

The lake was always cold, even on the hottest of summer days. As Cassidy laid her towel onto the grass, she wondered if she'd even be able dip a toe in today. Her goose bumps still hadn't gone away after her talk with Deb. Her bathing suit hugged her body under her shirt and shorts. Rose was chattering away on her cell phone by the trunk of one of the oaks. Ping and Joey arranged their towels and bags in partially shaded spots on the grassy make-shift beach. Both appeared stone-faced, thoughtful, afraid. Cassidy knew why; she felt the same way.

On the way out of the Estates, Rose had driven past the Chases' house. Police had been crowded around the driveway, where an ambulance was parked. Rose had slowed, and they'd noticed Mrs. Chase sitting in the back of the ambulance wearing a numbed expression even as a couple EMT workers and cops spoke with her. "Wonder if everything's okay," Rose had said, turning onto the main drag. None of the three had said a word in response. Cassidy couldn't help but remember Joey's map, how it had revealed that the old farmhouse now hiding in the woods up the hill had once stood on that very spot.

"Hey you guys," said Ping sitting on her towel, reaching into her tote bag and pulling out a copy of *Strange State*. She opened to a dog-eared page and spread out the magazine on her towel. "Check this out." Cassidy and Joey scooted over toward her. Ping pointed at an article titled "Mysteries of Whitechapel's Quarry Lake."

"Whoa," whispered Joey, leaning closer. "You just bought this, didn't you?"

Ping smiled. "Turns out that this whole area is a hotbed for *strange* activity. People tell stories that Quarry Lake is actually a bottomless portal to another dimension. Others say they've seen strange creatures swimming out in the middle of the water."

Cassidy's already weakened desire to hop into the water that morning instantly evaporated. "What kind of creatures?"

Ping squinted, reading. "Giant snakes. Fish with huge teeth. Humanoid things with great big hands that will pull you into the depths."

"Yeah, right," said Joey, sitting back on his heels.

"This is what this whole magazine is about. Folklore. Most of it's probably a load of bull. But there might be some truth mixed in somewhere."

"But people still swim here," said Cassidy, glancing out at the water. Never before had the placid surface seemed so ominous. She nodded at the few other people who had parked themselves on the grass all around them. "If there were monsters here, don't you think this place would be deserted?" *Like the area around Mrs. Chambers's house?*

Ping laughed. "Probably." She stood and waved for Cassidy and Joey to join her. "Let's prove the conspiracy theorists wrong." She dropped the magazine, then she took off, sprinting toward the water.

CHAPTER TWENTY-TWO

PING WAS ALREADY HALFWAY across the pond by the time Cassidy and Joey jumped from the grass into the icy water. It had always been a shock to Cassidy whenever she'd dropped straight down at the edge of Quarry Lake. Not only was the temperature jarring, but the rock was sheer even on this side of the water. There was no gradient to the shore, like at a beach. It had been dug out long ago, she imagined, by steam-powered cranes and dust-covered men with muscled arms. It was easy to imagine how stories spread about the water being bottomless. In the city swimming pools, where Cassidy had learned how to swim, you could see the tiled floor below. Here, if you looked down, you'd barely find your toes kicking at the ends of your legs, and beyond that, there was only the blackest black.

Joey splashed Ping who whooped and waved, but Cassidy was suddenly overcome with hints of those familiar bad feelings — the numbness, the headache, the disorientation — that came when the world seemed like too much. She scrambled back to the rocky ledge. And when she happened to brush her leg against a slimy part of the underwater wall, she yelped and kicked and splashed until she was lying safely upon the grass beside the shoreline, catching her breath, staring at the sky. When she blinked, she saw pale hands, wrinkled flesh, rising quickly through the watery dark.

She stood, shivering, glancing back toward her towel, her backpack, and the notebook she knew was inside. She wanted desperately to sit and write another entry, to lock her fright onto the safety of the page, like Levi had told her to do, where it was only a story, where it couldn't hurt her. Joey and Ping were in the center of the lake, treading water like pros. She knew if she refused to join them in their fun, her memories of Quarry Lake might be forever ruined.

Voices carry across water, so when Ping called out "What's wrong?" Cassidy heard it as if Ping were beside her.

She shouted the first thing that came into her head. "It's cold!"

Her heart pounded sludge through her chest as she thought once more about the *Book of Bad Things*. She inhaled a deep gulp of air, then jumped back into the water. Snakes, teeth, clutching hands. With every stroke she pulled, Cassidy shoved them down into the depths of the lake, into the depths of her mind. She would not allow the lake to become a bad thing either. With every breath she took, she felt lighter, weightless. Seconds later, she arrived at her friends.

"I thought you were gonna chicken out," Joey said, flicking droplets of water at her.

Cassidy grunted. "I'm not a chicken."

"Relax." He smiled. "I'm just pulling your leg."

Pale hands . . . Rising from the darkness . . .

With that, Cassidy kicked out at him, brushing his calf with her toe. When he screamed, wide-eyed, looking like a fool, she laughed and whispered back, "Relax. I'm just *kicking* your leg."

After a three-way splash attack, Cassidy realized that the panicky feeling had disappeared. And the stories that Ping had shared from the magazine were only stories once more. "So what else does *Strange State* say about Whitechapel?" she dared to ask. "What other weird things should we know?"

Ping mentioned a few other articles she'd come across within the past day: barren places in the woods where no birds would sing, caves that belched soot, huge boulders that were balanced impossibly upon a few small stones, and ancient tunnel systems that were supposedly home to feral children and their cannibalistic parents. By the time she finished recounting what she'd read, the trio had traveled nearly all the way to the base of the sheer rock wall that rose high over their heads.

"These places are all in Whitechapel?" Joey asked. "How come I've never heard of them?"

"They're not all in Whitechapel," Ping answered. "But they're nearby. I might even be able to point out most of them to you on that old map."

Feeling an ache in her limbs, Cassidy waved for the group to follow her as she ventured back across the water. "You still think you should write to the editors, Ping? Tell them about what's been happening by us in Chase Estates? 'The Mystery of the Moving Farmhouse.'"

"Yeah," said Joey. "That and 'The Ghost of the Hermit Hoarder.'"

Ping followed Cassidy. "I forgot to tell you guys that I asked my dad about the old Chambers house. How it could have ended up where it is now, and why."

"And?" Joey asked. "What did he say?"

"He'll do some research and get back to me. One of the benefits of having academics for parents."

Once they'd returned to their stuff, they toweled off and lounged in the grass, digging into the cooler that Rose had brought along for bottled water. To Cassidy's surprise, Rose was still on the phone, by the tree. Joey watched his mom, looking nervous as she paced back and forth. Something was wrong. The early-morning sirens echoed in Cassidy's mind.

She wrapped her towel tightly around her shoulders. After a few minutes, she slathered on some more sunscreen, then lay down out of the shadows' reach, to beat the deep chill radiating from her bones.

Rose told them what had happened, but only after Joey begged her when they were in the car, heading home.

Kitty Chase had found her husband's body on the floor of his office that morning. He was covered in nicks and scratches, as if he'd been attacked by wild animals. The police were confounded. The house had been sealed up. The alarms had been set. Strangest of all, Mrs. Chase claimed she'd found Owen's office crowded with taxidermy animals, items Owen had told her he hoped to trade at the auction house in the fall. A fox. An owl. A badger. A hawk. The group of stuffed creatures had been arranged in a macabre circle around Owen's body, as if they'd watched him die. As if they were the guilty party.

Cassidy and Ping huddled close in the backseat, their chests heaving at the shocking news. Up front, Joey sat stiffly and stared forward. Driving in silence, Rose must have been in a bit of shock herself, Cassidy figured, or else she might not have divulged such disturbing details to a group of twelve-year-olds.

Ping leaned close, whispering in Cassidy's ear, "He took those animals from the Chambers house. We saw him do it!"

Cassidy nodded, not saying aloud the questions that ran through her head. Did Ursula take something of his in return? His most valuable possession? Had she stolen his life?

Chapter Twenty-Three

Hours later, after dinner — pizza and salad — Joey's sister, Deb, drove Cassidy and Joey into town for the outdoor film. *Jaws* in the park.

On the way, Deb stopped to pick up her friend Julia. Once the two older girls were together, their conversation circled around the topics of jobs and movies and boys named Hal and Trevor and Billy and Calvin (with a brief digression into the town's recent deaths) and did not stop until Deb found a parking space at one of the already crowded public lots. Cassidy was almost glad that Deb and Julia had so much to catch up on; she wasn't sure what she would have said to Joey otherwise.

The four hauled blankets and folding chairs out from the back of the car and trudged up the hill in the direction of the crowd. The Whitechapel Parks Department had set up a screen on a large piece of lawn several blocks away from the town hall, where the roar of the churning rivers wouldn't interfere with the sound system. Cassidy imagined, though, that the sound of the meeting waters might only have enhanced the effect of the film. The lawn was already peppered with small groups of people who'd come out to enjoy the old movie while sitting under the stars, but Deb managed to find a spot in the center where they wouldn't have an obscured view.

Joey sat beside Cassidy and munched on the kettle corn that Rose had stuck in the picnic tote. Cassidy opened a can of ginger ale and took a swig.

The day's sun had baked the grass. The blanket was thick and warm underneath them. Deb and Julia sat just behind them in the low folding chairs, continuing their prattle, this time in whispers. The crowd around them was filled with others their age. Who knew who was listening?

Cassidy sat with Joey in silence, but she didn't mind that he was quiet. Now that she understood that Lucky's death had been weighing on him like a lead blanket, she felt better about the changes in their friendship. It didn't make everything okay between them, not in her opinion, but she was happy that at the very least, he hadn't refused to come along to the movie or to Quarry Lake that day. Strange, Cassidy thought, that it had taken several bad things — deaths and hauntings — to occur in order for him to see her as a friend again.

The sky was still blue, but night was coming up quickly, stars blinking to life above them. The notice in the paper had mentioned that the film would start at dusk.

"Hey, you guys!"

Recognizing the voice, Cassidy and Joey sat up and looked around. Ping stood several blankets back and was already hopping over people's outstretched feet as she made her way toward them. Cassidy and Joey waved. Leaping the last few feet toward their spot, Ping plopped down on the blanket between them. "Hi, Deb," she said quickly before turning back to her friends.

"You came with your family?" Joey asked.

Ping pointed in the direction from which she'd stumbled. Mr. and Mrs. Yu were busy trying to contain her two little brothers, who'd decided that a race around their own wide spot of lawn would be a fun way to pass the time until the movie began. "Aren't they a little young for *Jaws*?" Deb asked, glancing over her shoulder. Finally, Mrs. Yu noticed and waved.

"They're only two years younger than me. Mom says if they get too scared, they'll head home. If they do, can I catch a ride with you guys?"

"Of course," said Deb, waving back to the Yus, nodding at Ping and giving a thumbs-up.

"Cool," said Ping, settling onto the blanket, as if she were now part of a new family. She grabbed a handful of kettle corn and shoved it into her mouth. As she did so, she leaned in, whispered, and chewed. "I begged . . . my parents . . . to take me here after we ate dinner. I knew you guys were coming . . . and I had to see you tonight. When my dad got home from work, he told me about the Chambers house."

"What about it?" asked Joey, stiffening.

"How they moved it," Ping answered with a dark smile. "And why."

CHAPTER TWENTY-FOUR

PING EXPLAINED AS MUCH as her father had learned.

The map that Joey had found at Junkland was accurate. The old house that had once marked the entrance to Chambers Farm, where the Chase McMansion stood today, was indeed the same house that sat in the woods beyond their cul-de-sac. Fifteen years or so ago, when Owen Chase had offered to purchase Aidan Chambers's land, the old man had at first refused. Aidan had grown up in that house, he'd said. It was in his *blood*. Unfortunately, according to Chase's proposed design, the perfect geographical entry from the main road ran right through the property.

Aidan had been intrigued by the price Chase had offered, but insisted that he be allowed to keep his house and the parcel of land on which it sat. Mr. Chase had countered that they move the house up the hill, into the Estates themselves. Up in the woods, detached from the rest of the new houses, Aidan could maintain his privacy. Chase knew it would be an expensive effort, but if it was the only way to get Chambers to budge for the lot, it was worth it. Aidan took the bait. A year or so later, a group of contractors disassembled the old farmhouse and put it back together at the opposite side of the land that had been in the Chambers family for over a hundred years.

"That doesn't sound so mysterious," said Joey, disappointed. "Mr. Chase bought the land. They moved the house. Big deal."

"Right," Ping nodded. "But that's not all. According to my father, people around Whitechapel say that after the move, Aidan

Chambers became a different person. Suspicious. Frightened. They say he claimed that his house was now haunted."

"Why would moving a house up a hill make it haunted?" Cassidy asked.

"Maybe it wasn't the house that was haunted," Ping said. "Maybe it was the land that they put it on."

"Can *land* be haunted?" asked Joey.

"Anything can be haunted," said Cassidy, thinking of her own trip to the cemetery in Brooklyn years ago. She shifted her weight on the blanket. "And according to the stories, both Aidan and Ursula seemed to change once they lived in that old house in its new location. Right?"

Ping nodded as Deb chimed in from behind them. "I remember when Ursula first came to the neighborhood." The three on the blanket flinched, unaware that she had been listening. "You're right, Cassidy. She was a different person. Very sweet. Generous. I was really young, but I remember her coming over, chatting with mom and dad. I think, once, she even babysat us."

"She did?" Joey said, aghast.

"But she changed. Stopped talking to people. Stopped leaving her house. It was really weird."

"She lost it," said Julia, looking up from her phone. She'd interrupted her text message to chime in. "You guys saw what they pulled out of that house this week. Would a sane person have lived that way?"

Everyone was quiet for a moment. The sky was growing purple now, the stars creating a light show unlike anything Cassidy ever saw in the big city.

"It's complicated," Joey answered quietly.

"I've heard stories," Julia added, her eyebrows raised. "Our friend Hal says he's seen Ursula every night this week."

Cassidy turned around and grabbed Julia's ankles. Julia squealed in surprise. "Hal who?" Cassidy sputtered. "What has he seen?"

"Hal Nance," Julia said, chuckling. "Deb's boyfriend."

"He's *not* my boyfriend," Deb said. "We went on one date. *Last year.*"

"Anyway," Julia went on. "He's seen her ghost too. He said she seemed really mad that he took something from her house. What if all that junk is cursed?"

Cassidy remembered the dark-haired boy she'd talked to in the supermarket last Monday, the one who'd let her use his phone. His name had been Hal. She blinked and saw him lying in a coffin, his skin tinged pale blue, his voice ringing impossibly in her ears: *Too late, too late, too late.*

"You have to call him now!" Cassidy said. "Tell him he has to put back whatever it was he took!"

Julia laughed and Cassidy blushed. Julia held up her phone, revealing her past few texts. "Tell him yourself," Julia said. "He's just getting off his shift at work. He said he'd stop by here and watch the movie with us for a bit."

"He did?" Deb asked, flipping her hair over her shoulder as if trying to look like she didn't care, though it was obvious she did.

"Maybe," said Julia, glancing back at her phone, as if a new text would spring up and provide an answer.

Just then, the screen at the front of the lawn lit up white and a voice rang over the speaker system. "Welcome to Whitechapel's Movie under the Stars!" The crowd, who'd grown substantially since Cassidy had last looked around, roared with applause. "Tonight, we've got a classic," said the announcer, a man wearing a green parks department T-shirt standing at the edge of the screen holding a microphone. "A real scary one."

Cassidy promised herself that when Hal showed up, she'd make him listen to her, even if she had to drag him to his car and drive him up to Ursula's house herself.

The man by the movie screen laughed evilly, hamming it up, adding, "I wanna hear you all scream!"

A few minutes later, the movie started, and for the next couple hours, the audience obliged his request over and over and over.

HAL NANCE STROLLED across the parking lot, his eyes fixed on his car, an ancient El Camino that several generations of extended family had fixed up and handed down in a line that had last year brought the keys into his own hands. He loved the car, even though, according to most anyone who saw it, it was strange looking. The two-seater had a pickup bed in the back, like a truck, which Hal found useful for carting around various things for his friends and family. Within the past few weeks, he had carried a pair of amps for Ted Walsh's band's gig a couple towns away, a couch that his mom was donating to a local church charity, and a new barbecue grill his dad had purchased at the home and garden center by the highway.

The current cargo, however, was weirder — an antique sewing mannequin, a female torso made of cardboard and pressed tin attached to a wooden stand with four little rolling wheels at the base. He'd taken it from a dead-end driveway at the crest of Chase Estates that week, planning to use it in an art project. Now, the thing sat in the back of the El Camino for no other purpose than Hal had wanted to get it out of his house and hopefully out of his life.

He checked his watch, but the indigo sky was the true indicator of time. The movie must have started by now.

As he approached the car, the form seemed to glow beneath the phosphorescent light high above the parking lot. He could not stop himself from imagining how very much it looked like a dead body. He'd almost hoped that someone would have stolen it during his shift, but no such luck. He slowed, not wanting to be so close to it, and remembered the strange visions he'd had since visiting the Dumpsters in Ursula's driveway.

His pocket buzzed, and he jumped. Hal pulled out his phone and glanced down at the screen. A text from Julia Freundlich. He sighed and tucked it back into his pants. He'd promised her that he'd stop by the movie they were showing in the center of town, but seeing the mannequin again now propped in the back of his car, as if waiting for him, only made him want to stick with his original plan: to drive the creepy old thing back up to the driveway and leave it there, like the old woman had asked him to.

Hal had been visited by Ursula on the night he'd taken the mannequin home. He'd woken to find her standing at the end of his bed, next to the dressmaker's tin dummy, one clawlike hand resting on its shoulder. He'd scrambled backward against the wall. At first, he figured that what he was seeing was a dream, but the vision didn't fade. Though she was transparent, she wore what looked like a faded jogging suit. Her wide eyes were black and imploring, her mouth sagged, her lips moved as if she were about to speak. Sadness and anger and frustration crowded into the room like smoke, and Hal nearly choked. As soon as he'd spoken — "What do you want?" — Ursula's form disappeared like condensation wiped from a mirror. But the mannequin remained.

Even after Hal moved the dummy into the hallway outside his room, he hadn't been able to find sleep again.

He'd never planned on telling anyone that he'd seen her ghost, but the next day, he heard others' stories. People who'd visited the Dumpster were claiming that Ursula Chambers had come to them at night, demanding they return what they'd taken.

Hal hadn't been sure what Ursula had tried to say to him, but he allowed himself to believe her appearance had been a warning.

By the next afternoon, he felt comfortable enough to share his own tale with a familiar customer. Julia Freundlich, who was running the register next to his, had overheard him. That was all it had taken for Hal to become one of *them*: Those Who Had Seen.

Later, driving home, he'd found himself laughing about what had happened and what others were saying. Curses? Ridiculous. Then Mrs. Moriarty died, and his humor dried up.

So, before work, he'd thrown the dummy into the bed of the El Camino. This evening, he intended to drive up to the overgrown driveway where he'd gotten it. Maybe he'd even roll the thing to the rotting porch and leave it there, just to be rid of it, just to be safe.

Now, Hal yanked his key from his pocket and shoved it into the car door. If he drove quickly, he might make it back to the center of town before the scene when the shark chomps the kid on the raft, the blood bubbling in the surf.

Hal chuckled to himself as he slipped behind the wheel, thinking about how the horror of the film should not be a comfort. But when he thought about the moment the kid's mother slaps Chief Brody's cheek in anger, he nearly forgot about what was sitting in the car's bed right behind him or where he needed to drive to dispose of it. Anything distracting was a comfort at this point. He slammed the door shut and turned the key in the ignition. The engine purred to life.

Pulling out of the parking lot and onto the dark road that led over the hill toward Whitechapel, Hal wondered, not for the first time that day, if he was overreacting. People in small towns told small stories — a side effect of being bored, nothing else to do but gossip about the woman who lived in a pile of junk, like a character from a nursery rhyme. Maybe the plan was a bad idea. Maybe he should just go into town and watch *Jaws* with the girls. Forget about the rumors. About the dreams. Nightmares. He'd felt guilty for taking what didn't belong to him. But that didn't mean he or anybody else in Whitechapel was *cursed*, did it?

Hal switched on the radio but couldn't get a signal. Every station emitted an odd humming noise. It wasn't static. It was like a hundred voices singing out of tune. He glanced into the rearview mirror, but he couldn't see the mannequin. Had it slipped out of sight, fallen flat on the bed? Reaching up, Hal adjusted the mirror. Now, somehow, the dummy was sitting upright in the pickup bed, as if its stand had folded at the hip. If it had a head, it would have been glaring at him.

He slammed his foot against the brake and the car skidded, the tires screeching into the night. A scream of rubber against asphalt. The mannequin slid forward, smashing into the rear window, spidering a crack across the glass.

Pulling over to the side of the road, a line of dark trees easing up the steep hill, Hal spat out some choice words for his passenger, then swung open his door and leapt out into the street. "I don't need this. . . ." he said, tossing the broken pieces of the mannequin to the side of the road. "Good riddance." He wiped his hands on his jeans, a job well done, then hopped back into the El Camino and pealed out. Hal Nance was on his way. Back on track. Everything right with the world.

The night whipped by. Hal felt like an elephant had been lifted from his chest. He fiddled with the car radio again, but the humming sound only grew louder. He turned the knob furiously. But there was nothing else coming in.

Oh, who cared!? *Jaws* awaited. *Jaws* and Julia and Deb and the stars above. Tonight would be fun. No more worrying about evil hoarders from beyond the grave. Tonight was about sharks. Sharks and girls. And driving fast to get there.

Someone was standing in the road at the top of the hill. As soon as Hal saw her, he knew who it was. He slowed but didn't stop. When he got closer, he made out details: the jogging suit, the short, messy hair, the black holes where her eyes should have been, the open mouth, the moving jaw. He pressed his foot against the gas. He didn't want to hurt her; he only wanted her to leave him alone. The woman didn't move. As he passed through her, static burst from the stereo speakers and a voice screamed at him, *Go back! Go back! You must go back!*

Hal swerved to the side of the road, coming to a stop beside a great pine tree. He opened the car door and glanced back up the hill, at the spot where the woman had stood, trying to block his way. *Go back,* she'd said. The passage was empty now. An ordinary country road.

He looked ahead into the small valley below. The lights of the town filtered up through the trees, misty beacons leading the way to safety. He was almost there. All he had to do was drive. But Ursula's desperate plea was stuck in his head.

There was something about it that didn't match the stories people had told. If he could allow himself to process what he'd just seen as something that existed outside of a dream, then yes, her words were a warning. However, they didn't sound to him like a threat.

Hal sighed as he turned the car around. He drove slower now, keeping a lookout. Soon, he noticed a dull glimmer in the brush — his headlights reflecting off the rusted trim. The mannequin was waiting for him. And, if he understood properly, Ursula needed him to bring it back to her house. No matter what. He stopped. Got out. Knocked the broken glass from the window into the truck bed so he could see through the rearview mirror. He threw the dummy into the back of the car.

The town was deserted. Everyone was up the road and around the bend at the movie. He'd just passed the white chapel and the bridge over the river when the radio grew louder again. That humming noise. It battered his eardrums. Hal switched the radio off. But the noise didn't stop. It only increased. He felt a rumble in the pit of his stomach, as if he'd eaten a handful of gravel. "What the —" Hal flicked the knob back and forth several times before he realized that the humming, the vibrations, were not coming from the El Camino's speakers, but from outside.

His spine turned into a stone pillar as he thought of the dummy in the bed, how it had sat up in the hills before town. He'd smashed out the broken glass so he could see through the mirror into the rear, but now, he had a feeling that he didn't want to see what was back there. And yet, as the humming became so strong it threatened to boil his brain, he knew he had to look.

Once again, the mannequin sat upright. In the ambient light from the dashboard and what was left of the moon above, Hal made out some movement surrounding the object. A dark patch, an obsidian roiling shadow, hovered in the air over the mannequin before swarming forward to embrace the female form with snake-like tendrils.

Hal felt something squeezing at his throat, and he realized he was screaming. Still, he couldn't tear his eyes away from the nightmare in the rearview. The mannequin now appeared to have a head made of the shadow stuff. Its long hair blew back from its scalp, whipped up in a frenzy of backdraft, and its face . . . Well, it had no face. Two arms extended from where its shoulders had once simply cut off, now reaching toward him, hands stretching from what looked like black mist, solid fingers whittled into impossibly sharp talons.

By the time Hal realized that the mannequin had breached the broken window, its claws about to slice at his neck, he'd already veered off the road. Slamming on the brakes did nothing. The El Camino's tires slid in the dew-slick grass. Ahead, the trunk of a wide oak grew blinding white as the headlights approached. At the last second, as a sharp pain pierced the flesh of his neck, Hal managed to twist the wheel. This did little to stop the car from careening forward, except to spin the vehicle so that it collided with the tree from the side instead of the front.

In the instant before his waking world blinked away, Hal's last thought was, *Ursula's going to be so mad at me.* . . .

CASSIDY'S BOOK OF BAD THINGS, ENTRY #9:
NIGHTMARES

Imagine you're walking along a beautiful mountain path, surrounded by everyone who loves you. Janet and Benji are beside you, holding your hands. You don't know why you've all ended up on this hike, but it doesn't matter. Nothing matters except taking the next step, finding your balance, making your way into the clouds. You get to a point where the path is steep and unclear. No one knows whether to step up onto a rock or down into a gully. The next thing you know, you've lost your grip on your best friends' hands, and you watch as they tumble down the mountain, bouncing as their bodies collide off each other and the rocks, coming to rest on the ground far below. And you know they're dead.

   Then you wake up.

Imagine that you're following your father into a brightly lit parking garage. He wants to show you his brand new sports car. Together, you'll drive off with the top down into the night, speeding through city streets, the wind messing up your hair, but you don't care because of the thrill. You find yourself standing at the back of a red Porsche. A voice behind you tells you to open the trunk. So you do. Inside, the space is empty and padded with black felt. Then, the voice behind you says, "Get in." You turn around and realize that you haven't followed your father. You've followed someone else. Someone you don't recognize. Someone with big hands and an even bigger smile.

   Then you wake up.

Imagine that you're taking swimming lessons at the local YMCA. You're not a bad swimmer, so you have no problem when the instructor asks you to demonstrate your ability to the rest of the class at the deep end of the pool. In fact, you beam with pride. Everyone applauds as you adjust your goggles onto your eyes then leap as far as you can into the middle of the pool, through a square-shaped hoop. Under water, you realize you haven't jumped through a mere hoop. Bars surround you, and you understand that you're in a cage. Glancing up, you see the bars have locked you in. You're now wearing scuba gear. You can breathe. But you're confused, because this isn't what your instructor has asked you to do. Then, through the blue haze beyond the bars, you see dark shapes swimming toward you. At each wall of the cage, large mouths open, great white sharks who've marked you as dinner. You scream, a burst of bubbles that no one at the edge of the pool can hear. You try not to panic as you examine the cage for a way out. That's when you look down and see the bottom is completely open. And rushing up from the darkness is an open mouth, an entrance to a tunnel of hunger. Pink globs of meat are stuck between razor-sharp white teeth, remnants of the shark's last meal. The one before you.

Then you wake up.

I think the scariest nightmares are the ones where everything is normal, pleasant even, then snap, the world turns and shows you how truly frightening it can be.

Our brains are so mean.

CHAPTER TWENTY-FIVE

THE MORNING AFTER *Jaws*, Cassidy was lying in bed, her eyes closed, her brain bouncing between sleep and wakefulness, when she heard the door squeak open. "Joey," Cassidy mumbled, turning over, clutching the blanket at her chin. "It's so early." But Joey didn't answer. Her consciousness tilted back toward dreaming, even as she felt cool skin against her wrist. A soft grip took her palm, and at first, Cassidy struggled to take back her hand. But the grip was insistent. It pulled her harder, so hard in fact, that Cassidy felt her shoulder pop.

"Oww," she said, sitting up, still unable to remove herself from the grip. The room was almost pitch black. It was even earlier than she'd thought. Cassidy could not see who held her, but she knew it was not Joey. Ragged breathing filled the darkness. Cassidy was suddenly freezing. "Who's there?" she asked, unsure she wanted an answer.

Cassidy felt herself sliding over the edge of the mattress, so she swung her feet to the floor and with her one free hand, pushed herself up. Before she could gain her bearing, the person pulled her toward the bedroom door.

Only when they were both outside, walking up the street toward the overgrown driveway at the end of the cul-de-sac, was she certain whom she was following. Though she expected to feel afraid, mostly, she felt a sad emptiness.

Ursula Chambers was Cassidy's height. Her short hair was tightly curled. She was dressed in her legendary jogging suit. Out in the night, the woman was transparent phosphorescence, glowing dimly like starlight. And though Cassidy could still feel the dry coolness of Ursula's skin, there was an icy chill underneath it, like a sickness, a fever.

They stood on the front steps of Ursula's old house. Inside, the sound of claws scrabbled on the rough wooden floor. Cassidy tried to back away, but the old woman held her still. Reaching forward, Ursula pushed open the door. Beyond the threshold, Lucky sat and stared at Cassidy, smiling that big goofy grin of his. His coat was shining and clean, tinted slightly silver now, different from his usual blonde.

Cassidy almost burst into tears. This was not the same dog she'd seen limping up the road at the beginning of the week, no more than the woman in the gown had been Ursula . . . or *this* version of Ursula, at least. Cassidy could feel the difference between what she'd witnessed on Monday night and now. Despite the fever-chill of Ursula's touch, she knew there was safety in this dream version of the Chambers house. Only in the world of the awake, with that humming sound that trembled the very ground, had the apparitions contained malevolence, a poison.

Ursula turned from the house and looked at her with a smile, as if she could hear Cassidy's thoughts. Then, as if in answer, Cassidy heard the old woman's voice, a touch of Irish brogue, whisper, "Please, come in. . . ."

Then Cassidy woke up.

When Cassidy opened her eyes, her room was lit dimly with the beginnings of the day. She raced down the hall to Joey's room, knocking quietly so as not to wake the rest of the house. Seconds later, she heard a rustling sound. The door opened slightly. "What is it?" Joey asked, his voice crackling.

"We've got to go to her house," Cassidy said. When Joey widened his eyes and shook his head, she added, "You, me, and Ping. Today. There's something Ursula wants us to see."

CHAPTER TWENTY-SIX

A FEW HOURS LATER, Cassidy sat on the front steps of the Tremonts' house, kicking the bottom stair with the heel of her sneaker. She was waiting for the first stirrings from the Yu house next door, so she could tell Ping about her dream. It was still too early to knock.

Presently, she regretted knocking on Joey's door. He'd practically laughed in her face when she'd told him. "Are you insane?" he'd said, pulling her into his room, closing the door. "Don't you remember what happened the last time you suggested we go over there?"

Now, Cassidy wondered if she *was* insane. Had her vision of Ursula merely been a dream? A nightmare? Joey hadn't needed to remind her what was happening to the people the old woman had visited during recent nights.

But if there was a pattern here, Cassidy should be safe. She hadn't taken anything from the house. And Ursula hadn't presented her with a threat. She'd offered an invitation. Even so, without Joey to accompany her up the street, she wasn't sure she could go through with it. Ping was her last hope.

Something in her gut told her that if she sat by and did nothing, bad things would keep happening — and not only to the citizens of Whitechapel. She'd seen the trucks take away the overflowing Dumpsters a couple days ago. Who knew where that stuff might end up? Maybe a landfill . . . Maybe a thrift store . . . Maybe a classroom. Whether or not Ursula's ghost was the *thing* exacting revenge on the supposed thieves — and Cassidy wasn't entirely sure about that anymore — Cassidy knew that the answers were in that house.

The sky was brightening into a royal blue. Cassidy rose from the steps and walked out to the street. She stared at Ursula's overgrown driveway. A slight breeze crept out of the woods, rustling the leaves and vines and weeds.

"Whatcha doin' out here?"

Cassidy jumped, even as she recognized Ping's high-pitched voice coming up the street from behind her. She turned and smiled. "Waiting for you, actually. I figured you'd crawl out from your cave eventually."

"A cave!" Ping guffawed. "I'd like that, kinda. Actually, I came out looking for you too. Something happened again last night. Something not good. Have you heard?"

"Heard about what?"

When Ping got home, her parents told her a story. Halfway through the movie, the twins began complaining of mosquitos, so the Yus headed home. Far from the road, off in the middle of a field before Chase Estates, the flashing lights of rescue vehicles illuminated a disturbing scene. A car had lost control and hit a tree, its metal body wrapped nearly around the trunk.

"*Hal,*" said Cassidy, blushing. "Julia and Deb's friend never showed up last night."

Ping's pursed lips told her she was right. "He'd seen Ursula too."

Cassidy thought of the boy's kindness at the beginning of the week, when he'd let her borrow his phone at the supermarket. *Hal Nance is dead.* She was immediately nauseated. She swallowed hard, keeping her cereal down. Her eyes stung. "It's not fair," she managed to squeak out before her cheeks were wet. "I wanted to tell him to . . ." But Ping already knew what she'd wanted to tell him. It was too late.

Ping sighed and watched Cassidy cry. After a while, she took her arm, and they walked farther into the cul-de-sac, stopping in the center of the asphalt circle. Cassidy told her about the dream of Ursula and Lucky and the house, about what she thought it meant. Ping practically skidded to a stop, shaking her head. "You want to go *in there?*"

"We have to. People are dying. What if there's something we can do to stop that?"

"What do you think we'll find inside?" Ping asked. Then, wide-eyed, she squeaked out, "What if your dream was a trick? A trap?"

"And what if it was just a dream?" Cassidy asked, her face flushing. "What if all this is coincidence?" She shrugged. "We'd have nothing to lose," she finished, trying to sound confident, steady, strong, even though she felt the opposite.

"Unless it *wasn't* a dream," said Ping. She blinked. "Unless everything you imagined is real."

A particularly strong gust of wind rocked the trees up the road, and branches rubbed against one another, creaking and cracking.

"If Ursula Chambers thought someone could do something to help her, in whatever way she needs help, why would she choose *me?*"

"Because she knows you're one tough *chica*," said Ping, nudging Cassidy's arm. She turned to the driveway, the shadows dancing without a care in the morning light. "Okay, so if we're doing this, what do we need?"

"Me," said a voice from the curb. The girls turned to find Joey walking purposefully toward them, arms swinging, face pale.

Chapter Twenty-Seven

Cassidy shook her head. "You changed your mind?"

"I was watching you two from my bedroom. If you're gonna go anyway, then I'm coming with you."

"You don't have to do us any favors," Ping said with a huff.

Joey stammered. "I — I know. It's just . . ." He blinked and glanced into Cassidy's eyes before quickly finding his sneakers. "None of us would be in this situation if it weren't for me." He swallowed, as if trying to choke down a dust ball. "If I hadn't been, you know, such a jerk lately." Cassidy wiped her cheeks, surprised. "For the past year, I've blamed you for something that wasn't your fault. What happened to Lucky . . . And since you've been back, you've done nothing but try to help me feel better. I know you believe everything I've seen and heard and that means . . . a lot. But none of this is worth risking your life. *I'm* not worth it."

Pins and needles brushed Cassidy's skin. She closed her eyes. It wasn't time for tears again. Not if they were preparing to walk up the shadowed path. "You're wrong, Joey. You're worth everything. But thank you for saying the rest of it." When she glanced at him, his eyes were wide. Pink returned to his pale cheeks. "But you're not the only reason I want to figure all this out."

The girls filled him in on what Mr. and Mrs. Yu had seen the night before. The car crash.

"We must have driven right past it," he said, trembling, shaken. He'd known Hal Nance ever since he could remember. "I didn't even notice."

"Why don't we tell someone what we know?" Ping asked. "Our parents? Your sister?"

"But what *do* we know for certain?" Joey answered, his voice growing stronger, steadier. "Look what all my storytelling has accomplished over the past year. Yes, I've made a new *friend*, Dr. Caleb, but my parents pay for me to talk to him every week, so he doesn't really count. And when I start saying, 'Ursula's ghost is killing people who stole stuff from her house,' I'm pretty sure he'll want to put me on some sort of medication."

"But you have *us* now," Cassidy suggested.

Joey smirked, a sad expression, and she understood. If the Tremonts thought that she'd become a bad influence, reverting their son back to his paranoid ways, they might ship her back to Brooklyn. And then what? She thought again of the trucks that had carted away the Dumpsters, of where all that junk might end up, of what might happen to the people who found it, brought it into their own homes.

"So we're doing this?" Ping asked, nodding toward the Chambers property. The dilapidated house was hidden far up the driveway, but when the breeze moved branches, they could see bits and pieces of its dark wood. It seemed to be waiting for them like an animal — some sort of predator, the Big Bad Wolf. Cassidy and Joey nodded at once. "When?"

"Let's go now," said Cassidy, glancing at the patch of shadow, the house in the woods. "I've just got to grab my backpack." *My notebook*, she meant. It was still her secret. Like a security blanket she should have grown out of years ago.

"And I'll find some provisions," said Joey. "A flashlight might help."

Inside, Cassidy dashed upstairs and grabbed the book from under her pillow. She shoved it into her otherwise empty bag, then made her way back downstairs. Ping and Joey stood behind the couch in the living room, where Rose was sitting watching the local news.

A reporter was describing the situation from the parking lot of the funeral home down in the center of Whitechapel, but Cassidy didn't hear her words. The headline gleaming at the bottom of the screen had caught her attention. *Body Thief Strikes Again.*

Rose leaned forward, her face held up by the palms of her hands. She shook her head then noticed the group gathered behind her. "That poor family," said Rose. "What kind of sick person would steal corpses?"

"What family?" Ping asked, her voice rising even higher than normal.

"Mrs. Moriarty," said Rose. "And her son-in-law, Owen Chase. Both of them were to be buried this week. But *poof,* they're gone! I can't imagine what Kitty is going through." To herself, she added, "I should make some stuffed shells for her. Something hearty. Comforting."

Ursula's body had disappeared in a similar fashion only the week prior, Cassidy thought, her muscles tightening reflexively.

Behind the couch, out of sight of Joey's mother, the trio stared at one another, unspoken questions hanging in the air. Before any of them had the nerve to speak them aloud, Joey announced, "We're heading outside, Mom. Gonna explore. Back in a little while."

"Good idea. You kids shouldn't be watching stuff like this anyway." Still entranced by the television, Rose didn't turn around. "See you all soon," she said quietly, as the group crept guiltily out the front door. Cassidy hoped Rose was right.

CHAPTER TWENTY-EIGHT

ONE BY ONE, Cassidy, Joey, and Ping each stepped over the curb onto what was left of Ursula's gravel driveway. The canopy of leaves overhead was so thick, it seemed as though they'd immediately jaunted into another season, another dimension where shadows ruled. Cassidy led the group, twisting and turning up the long path, trying to avoid the tall clingy weeds and any plants whose leaves were tinged a poisonous red.

About halfway to the house, they came across a busted tennis racket lying in the middle of the gravel. A few feet past it was an overturned tin box. Tools spilled out of it. Farther along, more objects were scattered — plates, forks, knives, frames, books. Gauzy dresses hung hauntingly from the crowded scrub branches.

They paused when the mess became too thick to easily step over without touching any of it. "You think all this stuff fell out of the Dumpsters when they carted them off a couple days ago?" Cassidy asked.

Ping shook her head. "I don't think so. I remember the driveway looking pretty clear yesterday." She blushed. "What?" she asked, as if the others had accused her of something odd. "I was curious so I checked, all right?"

"If Ursula's ghost has been warning people to return her things, maybe this is the result," said Joey. He glanced between the girls.

"They didn't even bring the stuff up to the house," said Cassidy. "They just threw it on the ground."

"They were too scared," said Ping, staring up the drive. "I don't blame them."

Ahead, the farmhouse sat in shadow, its dark shingles mixing with the gloom of the surrounding trees. The front yard was overgrown with thick green shoots and wild looking, ugly yellow flowers. A few choked saplings sprouted up from the ground near the house's crumbling foundation. An aroma of pine sap masked another scent — something rotten. Cassidy took a deep breath through her mouth so she wouldn't have to smell it. For a moment, she thought she heard that humming, the primal-sounding noise that had woken her on Monday night and had caused her to come to the moonlit window. The house looked like it had been abandoned for years. You'd never have known that someone had lived there just last week. You might have imagined, however, that the person who'd lived there had also died there.

"Come on," said Cassidy. "Can't stop now. Not here anyway." She hopped over the items that had become Ursula's trash. Or Ursula's treasure? It was difficult to tell the difference anymore. The others followed, as if playing a game, seeking islands of solid ground, gray gravel, so they wouldn't have to step on the objects.

At the bottom of the porch steps, they stopped. This might be their last chance to turn back. Cassidy almost hoped for a sign telling her to do just that. The previous summer slammed into her memory. She heard Ursula's voice screaming at Joey and her to leave or else — such a different tone than the Ursula from her dream. She felt suddenly cold, and she clutched at her arms, rubbing away the chill. From the corner of her eye, Cassidy saw Joey do the same, and she knew that he was remembering too.

"If people are being punished for stealing things from this house," he whispered, "then what about Lucky?"

"What do you mean?" Ping asked.

"I mean, if Lucky was the *first* victim, and I'm pretty sure he was, he didn't steal anything. He was just a dog." The hurt in Joey's voice was enough to bring tears to Cassidy's eyes again. The afternoon of the previous year blinked through her brain again and again.

"But he *did* steal something," Cassidy answered, tenderly. "Maybe 'steal' is the wrong word. But he took something from the house. Remember?"

Joey's mouth dropped open. "That blanket. He was tugging at it through the basement window. When Ursula shouted at us, he tore off a piece. Then we ran." He swallowed. "The blanket was the thing he choked on later that evening, after we tied him to the oak in my backyard."

"His body disappeared too," said Ping. "Just like Mrs. Moriarty and Owen Chase."

Joey nodded reluctantly. Turning to Cassidy, he said, "In your dream, he looked good. He looked happy. He wasn't a . . . a zombie?"

"Not at all."

"Ursula didn't *kill* him," Joey said with certainty. "The blanket killed him. It was what he'd taken from the house."

Cassidy nodded. "Ursula didn't kill the others either. Mrs. Moriarty and Owen Chase . . . and Hal."

"The old woman was crazy," said Joey. "But maybe she was only crazy because she lived *here*. In this house. This is a bad place." He glanced up the stairs where the front door stood ajar. "Can't you guys feel it?"

"You sure you still want to go in?" Cassidy asked, staring into the darkness beyond the crack in the door. She took Ping's hand and squeezed it. Ping squeezed back.

To Cassidy's surprise, Joey answered, "How else are we gonna know just how bad it is?" He climbed the steps slowly and stopped in front of the door. Glancing over his shoulder, he smiled, as if proud of himself. Cassidy sighed as she followed, pushing away the thought that Joey's smile was premature — a grin like that would only bring them bad luck.

CHAPTER TWENTY-NINE

THE BOARDS SQUEALED with each step. When the three stopped at the entry, Cassidy felt the porch sag under their weight. She kicked the door open, almost expecting to see Lucky in his new silver coat sitting a few feet inside, waiting like the good dog he'd always been. But the door hit the inside wall with a resounding crash that echoed through the empty space, and even if Lucky had been sitting there, he'd most likely have taken off into the darkness beyond — ghost or not.

"Sorry!" Cassidy said.

"If there's anyone *or anything* waiting inside," said Ping, "at least now they know we've arrived. To kick butt and take names."

"That's true," said Joey, "but was *warning* them really the best plan?" He pulled a thin flashlight from his pocket and flicked it on.

Cassidy felt her face burn. If any of them deserved to be snatched up first, she figured that at this point it was her. She stepped inside, hoping that she hadn't awakened anything. The air felt like an oven. That rotten smell was heavier now. Cassidy pinched her nose. The house was silent; if Ursula was waiting for them inside, she was sleeping the sleep of the dead. Joey and Ping wandered past Cassidy, chasing the beam cast by his flashlight. In addition to the beam's glow, a murky light filtered through the front door from outside, revealing details of the room in which they huddled. It was a boxlike foyer with peeling, water-stained walls. Wide doorways opened to darkness on either side. Another door stood in the far wall at the foot of a narrow staircase.

"Where do we start?" asked Ping, stopping next to the warped banister.

"Depends on what we're looking for," Joey answered.

"Light," Cassidy said, flicking her hand against the closest switch in the wall. There was no response. Glancing at the ceiling, she noticed the fixture was empty. No bulb. She stepped farther into the room and found the nearest window. It was covered with thick velvet drapes. She pushed them aside. Yellowed newspaper was taped over the glass. She tore the paper away. Daylight leaked into the space, revealing a barren square-shaped room. Cassidy didn't know what she'd expected, but it certainly hadn't been emptiness. Had the cleaning crew removed any and all clues that Ursula may have wanted them to find?

"You heard the girl," said Ping, moving through the room toward another covered window. "Let's give her some light."

The three stayed close together as they went through the house, pulling away curtains and tearing down newspapers. To try to get rid of the stench, they opened every window, every screen, leaned outside, and gasped for fresh air.

Each room they illuminated revealed only that the cleaning crew had been totally thorough. Cassidy grew anxious. If there was nothing to see here, then maybe the previous night's vision really had been nothing more than a dream. Had she placed her friends in danger simply because of her own overactive imagination? But what was the danger? Except for the curtains and a few rotting rugs, this appeared to be an empty house. Cassidy remembered an old saying about appearances being deceiving. She was overcome with a feeling that they should leave. If something *bad* did happen now, Joey would never forgive her for putting them in this situation again.

"Maybe we should go."

"But we haven't even checked upstairs yet," said Ping.

"We've come this far," said Joey. "And this isn't as horrible as I thought it would be. Actually, it's kind of cool, seeing inside. This would have been a really nice place to live."

"*Kind of cool?*" said Cassidy, raising an eyebrow. "Okay then. Let's be quick about it."

Upstairs was much smaller than downstairs — only a hallway, two small rooms, and a bathroom between them. It was much hotter up here. The three tended to the windows, and soon they were breathing more easily.

"Not much else to see," said Cassidy, just as she tripped over the upturned edge of a faded rug. She stepped quickly and caught herself on the wall.

"Careful!" Joey shouted from the bathroom.

"I'm fine!" Cassidy called back. She was about to kick the rug back into place when she noticed something marked on the floor underneath it. A yellow line? Bending down, she ran her fingers across the wide old boards. The line had not been drawn as she first thought, but carved into the wood. "Hey guys," she shouted. "I think I found something."

Moments later, Joey and Ping helped Cassidy pull the rug back against the far wall. A strange design made of lines and circles and stars lay beneath it. The deep circles had been carved where the lines intersected. The misshapen stars marked other parts of the floor. These were connected by more straight lines. Someone had worked the floor with a sense of purpose. But the purpose was totally unclear to the three of them.

"Are these some sort of *occult* symbols?" Cassidy asked. "Is it magic?" Even though she wasn't Catholic, she had a sudden urge to make the Sign of the Cross.

"I read somewhere that the star is an ancient pagan symbol for protection," said Ping. "But I'm not sure that's what the symbols here mean, with all these circles and whatnot." She shook her head. "It *is* familiar. I've seen this . . . configuration of shapes before. I'm just not sure where . . . or what it means."

"I feel like I've seen it too," said Cassidy. "In a dream, maybe?"

Joey stood, stepping back from the carving, pressing himself against a wall, trying to get a sense of the entire picture. Then he nodded. "We've all seen this before," he said, "but it wasn't in any dream."

"Then where?" Cassidy asked.

"My map," Joey said. "The one I found at Junkland. This is the same. See?" He swept his hand across the diagram. "It's an overhead view of Whitechapel."

CHAPTER THIRTY

"You're right," said Cassidy. "That line there is the road that bisects the valley. The star at the bottom must be Whitechapel."

"Or *the* white chapel," said Ping. "Or the intersection of rivers. Something . . ." She squinted at the carving as if a clue lay under its surface. When the others looked at her funny, she went on, "Look at the other stars. If this is a map, then they indicate the locations of certain places. Important places, maybe." She clapped her hands in excitement. The echo rang through the house. "Of course! I know why this looked familiar. Yes, it's just like Joey's map, but it's also like my magazines! Look at the stars. Where they're placed." She walked across the map, pointing at different spots marked by the five-pointed pentacles. "Here's Quarry Lake," she said. "And over there are the belching caverns. And I think the spot there is where that boulder stands balanced on those small stones. There are lots more points marked here that I'm not familiar with, but I'm pretty sure that's what these stars indicate. The *strange* places of New Jersey."

"And each star is connected by a straight line," said Joey.

"And each spot where the lines intersect is circled," said Cassidy, nearly out of breath. Her heart pumped as if she'd just run several city blocks. Was this what Ursula had wanted them to discover? The map under the rug. "There's definitely a pattern," she said, steadying her voice, "but what does it mean? Did Ursula carve this?"

"Maybe it was her uncle?" Joey asked. "Aidan."

"It makes me think of ley lines," said Ping.

"*What* kind of lines?" Cassidy asked.

"I read about them in —"

"Your magazine," he interrupted. "Yeah, we get it."

"You don't have to get snippy," said Ping, with a forced smile. "It's a good thing for us that I like reading *Strange State*. But, yes, I learned about ley lines in my magazine. From what I remember, a geologist or archaeologist in Great Britain came up with the term, like, a hundred years ago. He discovered that most of the ancient sites — castles and graveyards and monoliths — that are scattered around the island are connected by defunct roads and pathways. Some people think that there's something mystical about these hidden paths, and that they're especially powerful in the places where they meet."

"The circles," Joey said, as Ping's words began to sink in.

"The guys from *Strange State* pointed out that the same thing can be said about certain sites on our own continent, in our own area."

"North American ley lines?" said Joey.

"You said they believe the lines are mystical?" asked Cassidy. "In what way?"

"They create vortexes," said Ping. "Or is it vortices? Something like that. Places of extraordinary energy." The three glanced at one another, understanding now exactly what that meant. "There aren't too many of these intersections." Ping bent down, running her fingers over one small section. "But check this out. Almost all the lines on *this* map meet in one spot. It's the biggest circle of them all."

Joey and Cassidy, who had, until then, stayed off the map, strolled tentatively to where Ping was crouched. Joey turned his flashlight back on, illuminating the greatest intersection of lines, which the carver had gone over with his or her knife, deeper than any other place on the floor. "You know where this spot is, don't you?"

Cassidy felt faint. This whole morning, starting with her strange vision, had all been leading up to this moment. This discovery. "It's here," she whispered. She pointed down. "Where we're standing."

Ping nodded. "The biggest circle, the spot where all these *weird* stars intersect, is where Mr. Chase moved the Chambers house so he could build our neighborhood. They accidentally placed the house right on top of what might be the largest vortex in this area. Maybe in the whole state." Then she blushed. "That is, if you believe in this sort of thing."

Chapter Thirty-One

Outside, a gust of wind picked up, creaking the branches of the old trees surrounding the farmhouse. Cassidy listened carefully for the sound of birds or bugs or frogs and realized that all these creatures must have known, somehow, to stay away from this place. Something had led her here, but now she felt a sudden and overwhelming urge to leave.

She had backed toward the bedroom door, was ready to turn and run, but Joey went on. "Let's assume, at this point, we *do* all 'believe in this sort of thing.' What does it have to do with what's been going on in Whitechapel? With the appearance of Ursula's ghost? With the deaths? The *missing bodies*? I mean, do I sound insane asking if these occurrences could all be the result of this . . . this vortex thing? The ley lines and all the rest of it? What is a vortex anyway?"

"Maybe we can look it up at home," Cassidy suggested, easing away from the others. She'd started to feel that old nauseated sensation that came with her panic attacks. With one hand, she held onto the doorframe to steady herself, and with the other, she clutched the strap of her backpack, inside of which was her notebook. She had to stop herself from pulling the book out and clutching it to her chest.

"I can tell you what I know," said Ping, standing her ground, unaware of Cassidy's growing anxiety. "Think of a vortex as a whirlpool. Or as a black hole. It's a spot where matter — *stuff* — spins to a central point. A vortex draws things toward its center. It keeps them there."

"Like how Ursula wished to keep all her stuff here in the house?" Joey asked.

"Exactly," said Ping. "Except . . . maybe it wasn't *Ursula's* wish."

"What do you mean?" asked Cassidy, stepping farther back, across the threshold and into the upstairs hall. "No one else lived here with her."

"What I mean is," said Ping, extending her arms, indicating the carvings at her feet, "maybe it was something else. Something bigger than Ursula Chambers. Bigger than Aidan. Older."

"Maybe," said Joey, his voice rising with excitement, "whoever created this map knew that. Either Ursula or Aidan had figured out that something was wrong with this house. Or, if not the house, then where the house was built. Both of them were . . . troubled while living here. Maybe this map was their way of putting some of these pieces together."

"Then why go to the trouble of carving it onto your bedroom floor? Why not just write it down?" Cassidy asked, pondering her notebook again. "Paper works just fine for me."

"They must have had a reason," said Ping. "If we can figure it out, maybe we can figure out the mystery of what's been happening in this house, of what's been happening to this town."

"Great," said Cassidy, turning and heading into the hall. "Then let's go and think about it at home."

At the top of the stairs, with Joey and Ping close behind, Cassidy felt immense relief. A pale glow from the open front door spilled across the foyer, inviting her to race down the steps and down the driveway, to escape into the comfort of true daylight. "Wow," she started, "I can't believe we actually found —"

But before she took the first step down, a sound echoed from somewhere beneath them. It sounded like the whine of an animal. Joey shushed her. "What's that noise?" he whispered.

Cassidy clutched at the railing, but let it go when she felt the whole thing wiggle away from the wall. She brushed her dusty hand off on her shorts. Carefully, they made their way down to the foyer, listening closely for the noise, but it didn't come again. Not right then. Instead, a bark came from below. This was followed by a soft tapping, like claws on concrete, that drifted up through cracks in the weathered floorboards.

"Now *that*, I heard," said Ping. "There's a basement!"

"I think we got what we came for," said Cassidy. "Maybe we should . . ."

But Joey had already turned into the hall opposite the front door, away from the exit.

"Hold on," she tried, reaching for him, but when she heard Joey whisper "*Lucky*," she knew she couldn't stop him.

Down the hall, Cassidy and Ping found Joey standing in the dark before another door, one that they hadn't noticed before. He pointed his flashlight at the knob. Right above it, a broken hinge was twisted. A padlock lay on the floor.

"What the . . ." Ping whispered.

"Was Ursula keeping something locked up?" said Joey, his voice harsh. He reached out and touched the knob. The door swung inward slowly, surprisingly quiet.

"Are you crazy?" said Cassidy, grabbing his arm. "Don't." Joey flashed the light in her eyes, startling her into letting him go.

"Cassidy," he whispered, serious. "You dreamed my dog was in this house. I *have* to do this. You *know* I do." Then he stepped forward into the dark.

CHAPTER THIRTY-TWO

A PLATFORM REACHED OUT a few feet beyond the door. From there, a set of steps descended. Cassidy watched in horror as Joey's flashlight bobbed and swung down into Ursula's basement.

"Lucky?" Joey called.

Ping tugged her hand. "We can't let him go alone."

"This isn't what I meant when I said we needed to come here. I never *dreamed* about the basement."

"Did you dream about the bedroom?" Ping asked. When Cassidy's face fell, she added, "See? Come on. There might be more that we need to know."

"Fine," Cassidy whispered. The light was now at the bottom of the stairs. She stepped forward if only to be closer to it. "But at the first sight of that dog, I'm so out of here. I don't care how happy he is to see us."

The girls skittered down the steps. At the bottom, they nearly barreled into Joey. He'd stopped short, looking in awe at the room. He moved the light slowly around the space, examining every inch. Cobwebs hung from the rafters. Mold and mildew dripped down the walls. But the basement was empty; if there had been anything here, the cleaning crew had removed it.

"Weird," said Ping. "It looks . . . new."

"New?" Cassidy said, wrinkling her nose. "More like filthy."

"I just mean, I thought a centuries-old farmhouse would have a basement made of stone. And mortar."

"This part of the house isn't *that* old," said Joey. "When they moved the building, Mr. Chase's company probably poured a new foundation. Concrete."

"Then why is that area all messed up?" Cassidy pointed to a dark spot on the wall across the room. The concrete had crumbled. A large crevice rose from the floor almost to the ceiling. When Joey moved the flashlight to get a better view, they all gasped.

Moving closer, following the others, Cassidy could see that the crack was wider than she'd first thought. Maybe a couple feet. She hadn't been able to tell because in the dark she hadn't seen the garbage that had been shoved inside. From about ten feet back, Joey's light illuminated trash bags, crumpled boxes, papers, clothes, a doll, even a small chair. All of it filled every inch of the gap, from the bottom to top.

So the cleaning crew hadn't gotten all of it after all, Cassidy thought.

"What is this?" Ping asked.

"Could be the opening to some sort of passage," said Joey. "But it's been plugged up."

"If it is a cave, or a tunnel or something," said Cassidy, shivering in the cool darkness, "Ursula mustn't have wanted anyone to go digging around inside." Joey seemed to take this as an invitation. He reached out and poked one of the torn trash bags with the tip of his light.

"Can we leave?" Cassidy asked. "Please? I'm scared."

"We heard something down here." Joey was disappointed. "Where did it go, if not in there?"

Ping pushed at his shoulder. "You think your dead dog crawled into that crack in the wall, then pulled piles of garbage in after himself?"

"I dunno! All I know is what I heard."

One of the bags fell from the crack and tumbled to their feet. Cassidy was too shocked to scream. More pieces of detritus began to shift, spill forth, and roll toward them, as if something inside the space was moving around. The three scurried back, watching the wall in wonder, the glare from the flashlight reflected like from a giant eye.

After a moment, the movement stopped. Dust stirred, floating on invisible currents, illuminated by the white glow of Joey's light. "Lucky?" Joey whispered again. "Boy?"

A human hand burst forth from the crevice. Pale-purple fingers pushed through the rest of the garbage, opening and closing, searching for something or someone to hold on to.

Chapter Thirty-Three

There was no time to think. The three of them moved as a unit, turning toward the staircase. They dashed together with a singular purpose: to get the heck out.

Ping reached the stairs first, followed by Cassidy and Joey. Before taking the first step, Cassidy briefly turned back toward the crack in the wall. Joey had done the same, shining his light at the spot where the garbage was now spilling far out onto the floor. Someone was crawling on his hands and knees out from the crack and into the basement, crunching debris as he went.

Cassidy meant to continue up the steps behind Ping, but her body wasn't listening to her brain. She couldn't believe what she was seeing. The man glanced up at them from across the room. Cassidy screamed as his milky eyes reflected Joey's light.

"Mr. Chase?" Joey asked, as if expecting a response. *Oh, hi there, kids. A little help?*

The man hissed at them, a phlegmy sound that escaped from deep in his chest. He struggled to kneel, his body jerking spasmodically, before he grunted, rising almost accidentally to his feet. There was more movement at the wall behind him. Another pair of hands appeared and clutched at the edges of the crack; another person was trying to pull itself out from whatever space was inside.

Joey swung the light away, and Cassidy yelped again.

"Go!" shouted Joey, pushing her spine with the tip of the flashlight. Ping was at the top of the stairs already. She waved them forward frantically. Cassidy nearly tripped as she took two stairs at a time. Darkness nipped at her heels.

She and Joey burst through the doorway, falling to the floor at Ping's feet. In the hall, the flashlight rolled against the wall, stopping near the padlock they'd seen earlier.

Noises echoed up from the basement. Slithering. Scraping. Shuffling. Cassidy took Ping's hand and leapt up. Joey grabbed at the doorknob, lifted himself, then swung the heavy door shut. From downstairs, a bark rang out, and Joey groaned. *"Lucky!"* he cried, reaching for the knob again.

"No!" Ping swatted his hand away. "He's one of them." Cassidy and Joey didn't know exactly what she meant by that, but they began to work it out, listening as the barking grew louder, frenzied.

"The dead," Cassidy said to herself. "Mr. Chase. And I think that was Mrs. Moriarty behind him. They're here. In the basement. But how?"

A tap-tap-tap of claws raced across the concrete floor below and up the stairs. Something heavy slammed against the door, rattling the old wood on its hinges. What sounded like an animal whined and scratched desperately to reach them.

"Apparently they walked!" Ping squeaked.

"Lucky!" Joey cried out, louder this time. His gaze fluttered between the two girls, desperate. "What if he's only trying to escape? Like us?"

"You know that's not true anymore," said Cassidy. "This is more messed up than we could've imagined."

Ping bent down and picked up the padlock. She grappled with the loose hardware that was screwed into the wood just above the knob, swinging the hasp over the staple, then looping the open lock through. She pressed the padlock down, and it clicked into place. And when next the door shuddered, even though some of its screws had become loose, the hasp held steady. Ping said nothing before turning down the hall, sprinting toward the daylight that was shining from the front door.

Cassidy picked up the flashlight, then took Joey's hand. He continued to stare at the shuddering door, as if something wonderful might be waiting for him just behind it. She yanked his arm, pulling him out of his head. "We've got to go!" It seemed like such an obvious idea, but Joey still looked surprised.

Together, they ran, following Ping's path, but before they turned the corner toward the front door, they were halted by another scream. Ping's voice was eardrum piercing — full of honest, no-holds-barred, throat-scraping terror.

Someone was blocking the way out.

CHAPTER THIRTY-FOUR

PING HAD MADE IT HALFWAY through the small foyer and was now quickly backing away. When she bumped into Cassidy and Joey, she screamed again.

"Who is that?" Cassidy asked, but Ping didn't answer.

The group drew closer into a panicked huddle, and when Cassidy got a better look at the figure in the doorway, she understood Ping's reaction. It was a woman, another corpse, who might have stood about five and a half feet tall, except that she was missing her head.

The three clutched one another, watching as the headless woman appeared to watch them back. At the end of the dark hall behind them, the banging at the padlocked door grew louder, as though the dog had been joined by the dead people who had crawled out of the hole in the wall.

They couldn't stay here, but they couldn't move.

"Hold on," said Joey, his voice suddenly calmer. "It's just a dummy. Wheels on the bottom of a wooden stand. My grandmother kept one of those in her sewing room." He sighed. "A mannequin. It's nothing."

"*Nothing*," said Ping, "except that it wasn't there ten minutes ago."

"Wait here," he said, stepping forward.

The girls glanced at each other and rolled their eyes. They followed instead. As Joey approached the door, hands out, ready to push the dummy out of the way, another figure stepped out from the side of the door and clasped the mannequin's shoulders.

Cassidy raised the flashlight to illuminate the face. When the three saw who was now barring their exit, they fell over themselves trying to turn around and landed in a heap on the floor.

The face belonged to Hal Nance. His usually pale skin was bruised all over. One of his eyes was entirely red, filled with blood. He was dressed in a ratty gray T-shirt and dingy gym shorts. He moved like the dead had done downstairs — slowly, jittery, stiff. Was it possible that he had just now walked from the morgue to join the others in their new trash-strewn home in the basement?

Hal wheeled the dummy across the threshold, limping and groaning as the wheels squealed.

"Leave us alone!" Cassidy cried out, hating the hopeless sound in her voice.

"We'll hurt you," Ping hissed.

Joey sat on the floor, unmoving, staring at his old neighbor. Cassidy worried that he might have broken something: a bone, his mind. She tried to help him stand up, to pull him away as the Hal-thing stepped closer to them.

"Joey?" The thing's voice was raw, as if it hadn't been used in a while. It glanced among the three of them. "I heard screaming. I hid. I thought . . ." Its eyes rolled as its mind seemed to hiccup. "I don't know what I thought. What are you guys doing here?"

"Please," Joey whispered. "Don't hurt us."

The Hal-thing flinched. "Why on earth would I hurt you?"

"Because that's what dead things do?"

"Dead things? What dead things?"

The pounding at the door down the hall shook the whole house. Who knew how much longer the latch would hold.

"*Those* dead things," said Joey, glancing over his shoulder. "And you."

Hal looked confused. "I was in an accident last night. The doctors thought I had a concussion. I got out of the hospital this

morning and knew that I had to bring this stupid mannequin back
here," he said quietly, as if he couldn't hear or couldn't comprehend
the sounds from the basement, "before it tries to kill me again." He
shoved the dummy forward. It toppled to the floor just inside
the door.

Cassidy tried to make sense of what he'd just said, but nothing
in her brain was computing. She had to concentrate to breathe.

"Wait a second," said Ping. *You're alive?*"

"Barely," said Hal.

A cracking sound erupted from the doorway by the stairs,
wood splintering.

"Well . . . good!" said Ping. "Then you need to follow us.
Now." She pushed past him and stepped out onto the porch, waving for the group to join her. With a grim look, she added, "I
suggest we run."

Chapter Thirty-Five

THEY RACED DOWN the gravel driveway, no pausing this time to avoid poisonous plants or sharp sticks — there are worse things in the world than rashes and scrapes. The light-filled opening at the end of the dark driveway grew as they trampled weeds and the scattered items that had once belonged to Ursula Chambers.

When the three friends exploded forth from the shadowed path and onto the cracked asphalt of their own street, Cassidy was flooded with such relief, she actually started laughing.

And she couldn't stop, not even when, seconds later, Hal Nance half limped, half skipped out of the forest in their wake. In fact, the sight of him only made her laugh harder. She knew it was wrong. Nothing about this was funny. But it was like something inside wouldn't allow her to feel real emotion, the *correct* emotion.

Shaking with giggles, she pulled the straps of her backpack tight, then strolled over to the curb in front of the Tremonts' house, where she sat, trembling, snot running out of her nose, tears making everything blurry. Ping and Joey followed. They stared at her, worried. Hal stood in the middle of the cul-de-sac, peering back up the driveway, as if he expected something else to leap out of the woods after him.

"This doesn't feel safe," he called to them over his shoulder. "We need to get away from this place."

Joey glanced up at his own house. "We can't go inside. Too close. Plus, if my mom sees you, she's going to start asking questions that I don't know if any of us can answer."

"Same with my mom," said Ping, glancing next door. "And if my little brothers learn that there are *freaking zombies* in the basement of the Chambers house, nothing will stop them from wanting to see for themselves."

Cassidy thought about her tiny apartment in Brooklyn, a place she'd never truly considered *safe*, and even that seemed like a better option than hiding two doors down from the Hermit's. Too bad they had no way of getting there.

"We'll go to mine," said Hal, pointing down the street. "I'd offer to drive, but well, I don't have a car anymore."

The Nances lived around the bend, on the street that led directly to the main road. Their home was a big brick box with an attached three-car garage — a model that resembled many others in the neighborhood. Mr. Chase had only offered four options when his company had developed the land, none of which were anything like his own grand mansion.

"My parents are at work," Hal said, leading them to a kitchen that opened onto a living room with a high ceiling just like the Tremonts' house. "They told me they'd check in, see if I was still alive." He smiled a halfhearted grin. "Make yourselves at home, if you can. How about some water?"

"*We're* happy you're alive," said Ping, her voice so earnest, it sounded as if it might shatter. "My parents saw the wreck and assumed the worst."

Cassidy sat on the edge of the wide couch, shivering as if it were winter. She couldn't stop thinking about what she'd seen in Ursula's house. Forget the bizarre map carved into the bedroom floor; what they'd found in the basement would haunt her for years, if not the rest of her life. The whole incident had already started to feel as if it had been a dream. Dead Mr. Chase had crawled out of a crevice in the concrete wall, pushing his way through piles of garbage. Mrs. Moriarty had followed her son-in-law. Presumably, Lucky's corpse had done the same. And if the pattern fit, then Ursula herself might have been down there too, dressed in her funeral gown. But was the Ursula who had walked home from the funeral parlor the same Ursula who had pulled Cassidy out of bed to invite her into her home? Had the dream been a trap, meant to lure them into the house, to meet the dead in the dark of the cellar?

Cassidy held a cold glass of water, her knees pulled close together, her backpack still hanging from her hunched shoulders. Hal had handed the water to her without her noticing. She shuddered as she realized that the others were talking — had been talking for some time. She listened to Ping, who was sitting beside her, finish telling Hal what had happened in the house. She assumed that Ping had already mentioned what had brought them there in the first place. On the other side of the sofa, Joey sat, staring into space, lost in his head just like Cassidy had been.

"Joey?" Cassidy interrupted. "You okay?"

Joey blinked, then seemed to notice that he wasn't the only person in the room. "Yeah. Sorry. I couldn't stop thinking . . ." Ping and Hal waited for him to finish.

"About the house?" Cassidy added. "Me too." Her voice felt tiny. It was a struggle just to speak.

"And Lucky," Joey said. "I'm just . . . confused. I know all of it should tie together somehow. But right now, it all feels like a nightmare. Nonsense. You're not where you thought you were anymore, not *who* you thought you were."

Hal sighed. "I haven't told you about what happened to me yet," he said. "I'm not sure if this'll help make things clearer, or only more complicated."

"Only one way to find out," said Ping, trying to sound as resilient as ever.

CHAPTER THIRTY-SIX

HAL DIDN'T REMEMBER the accident. He told them how he'd woken up in the field having, by some miracle, been thrown from the vehicle before it collided with the tree.

Another driver had seen the crash.

There were flashing lights and sirens, intermittently illuminating the field, the stretcher, the ambulance, the crushed metal *thing* that had once been his car.

He remembered begging EMT workers to search for the dummy, to bring it with them, to stop off at Ursula's house before they went on to the hospital. They'd watched him like he had a serious brain injury, but the tests showed that he did not. And there had been *many* tests before they released him into the care of his father, who'd driven him home in silence.

That morning, by the time he'd walked back to the scene of the accident, the wreck had already been towed away. About twenty yards past the tree, the dummy lay on its side in the dirt. In the morning light, it seemed harmless — just another piece of junk that someone wanted to be rid of.

Hal fit the stand back inside the mannequin where it had separated the night before. One of the wheels was stuck, broken, but he managed to get the thing over to the curb. He pushed it up the road, limping into Chase Estates, through the labyrinth of streets, to the uppermost point of the development. To the cul-de-sac.

That was where he'd heard the screaming.

❖

"You were right," said Joey flatly. "That didn't help at all."

Ping nudged his arm. "Of course it helps. You can't solve a puzzle without all of the pieces. And I'd say we have plenty more now. We can finally see the bigger picture."

"Oh, I can tell you what the bigger picture is," said Joey. "Don't need puzzle pieces for that."

"And?" Hal asked.

"We're all totally screwed."

Chapter Thirty-Seven

Ping ignored him. "Let's start with what we know. According to the diagram we found carved into the bedroom floor, the Chambers house sits on a vortex. Those lines and stars and circles coincide with info from my magazines and Joey's map of Whitechapel."

"Yes," Joey said, sitting forward, "but what does it mean?"

"Getting to that. We know that a vortex acts like a whirlpool. Or like a black hole in outer space. A place where energy spins, creates force. Like gravity. What do we know about black holes?"

Late morning light spilled through the windows at the front of the Nance house. The air conditioner hummed outside. After a moment, Hal raised his hand as if the den were a classroom. "They drag objects into them, crush them. Keep them there."

Ping nodded. "So if a ley-lines vortex is like a mini black hole, it may act in the same way. It wants to pull objects close to it. *Keep them there.*"

Cassidy sat up straight, even as she sank deeper into the couch cushions. "Is that why Ursula never threw anything away?"

"The house wouldn't let her," Joey added.

"Maybe," said Ping. "I mean, lots of people all over the world hoard junk."

"My aunt, Jeanne, has this illness called OCD," said Hal. "Obsessive-compulsive disorder. Hoarding is a symptom. Jeanne takes medicine to control her compulsions, and she's doing just fine."

"It must be really difficult for her, though, dealing with that," said Cassidy, thinking of some of her neighbors back in the city, the ones she'd visited with Levi Stanton. "It's made me feel a little sick whenever I've heard someone in this town calling Ursula a nutso-freakazoid."

"I don't think Ursula had OCD," said Ping. "Either way, Whitechapel didn't treat her very kindly."

"She didn't treat Whitechapel very kindly," said Joey quietly.

"She was a victim," said Ping. "Whether it was a disease or just her personality. She carried a whole lot. Don't you think?"

"And I doubt Ursula had medicine to help her," said Hal. "She was alone and helpless and scared."

"Okay, so Ursula's a martyr." Joey threw his hands into the air. "But right now, we're missing the point. Our problems are all about her house."

"I think so too," said Cassidy. "It's the house. The house is doing bad things."

"It's the *vortex*," Ping corrected. "The house just happens to sit on top of it. Moved there by Owen Chase years ago, so he could build his estates."

"So, Ursula . . . and her uncle Aidan before her," said Cassidy, trying to work it out in her head as she spoke, "might have learned that to remove anything that had been . . . *claimed* by this vortex was a bad idea."

"Bad how?" Joey asked.

The air conditioner clicked off. The house settled into stillness.

"Something came for me," said Hal. "Something dark. And old. It manipulated that mannequin. It growled this primal-sounding noise. It made me see things, hear things. I wouldn't be surprised if Mrs. Moriarty or Mr. Chase experienced something similar before they . . . you know . . . died."

"So if it wasn't Aidan and it wasn't Ursula," Ping said, "maybe something else is inside the house. Inside the vortex."

"Maybe the vortex *itself* is alive," Hal answered. "Maybe it's . . . intelligent. Greedy. It wanted back what we'd taken from it."

"If it couldn't have the mannequin," said Ping, "it tried to take *you*."

The group was silent for a moment. "The dead," whispered Cassidy. "If we're right about the vortex, maybe somehow it got its claws into the bodies and brought them back in place of what they'd stolen."

"That's why Ursula hoarded," said Ping. "She knew how it worked. If you take something from the house, you die. It could be why Ursula, or maybe her uncle, had carved the map into the floor. One less piece of paper that had a chance to get out into the world. She or he could sort out that hypothesis safely."

"That all works," said Cassidy, "except that Owen Chase gave his mother-in-law, Mrs. Moriarty, the mirror she said Ursula begged her to return. Moriarty never set foot inside that place, and she didn't *take* anything. I think how it works is like this: If you *possess* what belonged to the house, or the vortex, you die."

Hal nodded, his eyes wide, excited. "Then, the vortex-thing reaches out and brings *you* back to replace what it lost."

"You mean, your *corpse*," said Joey, grimacing. "Your walking, rotting corpse . . ."

"Ursula kept that basement door padlocked for a reason," said Ping, slowly, quietly. "Maybe she'd seen it for herself, who knows how many times."

Joey flinched. "You mean, she'd been living with who knows how many zombies in her basement? Right up the street from all of us?"

"So the *ghost* that people have been talking about," Cassidy added, "is different from the *zombie-thing* I saw walking up the street. Ursula's spirit hasn't been trying to hurt people. She's been *warning* people. Telling them to bring back whatever they took from the house."

"That makes sense," said Ping. "I mean, if any of this makes sense, then that does too."

"Wait," said Hal, looking pale, "does bringing the object back to the house break the curse? Am *I* safe now?"

Ping pressed her lips together. "We'll have to wait and see."

"And what about us?" Joey asked. "Since we were in the house, are we safe anymore? Or have we been claimed? Cursed? Does the vortex-thing think it *owns us*?"

"We have to do something," said Ping. "We have to tell someone what's going on."

"Who'll believe us?" Joey asked. "Not my parents, that's for sure."

"But they'll have to believe us when we show them what we've seen."

Cassidy cleared her throat. "But how can we bring anyone back to that house, knowing what we know now? If the four of us have been cursed, or *claimed*, simply by stepping inside the place, we can't allow that to happen to anyone else."

"What about the cleanup crew?" Ping suggested. "The Dumpster men. They've been inside the Chambers house. Maybe they've seen things too. Maybe they can help us."

"But how do we track them down?" Joey asked. "We don't even know the name of the company."

"Let's look it up," Hal said, getting up from the rocking chair and heading to a small desk in the corner of the room where a Mac console sat, its sleep light glowing from its glossy white front. He tapped the space key, and the screen came alive.

The talk of curses sparked something in Cassidy's memory, and she slipped her backpack off her shoulders. As the others continued to confer, she pulled her notebook out and flipped through the pages. Moments later, she discovered what she was looking for.

CASSIDY'S BOOK OF BAD THINGS, ENTRY #25:
CURSES

Different cultures all over the world have histories of curses in their folklore. In fact, there are several different words for curses, even here in the United States. Jinx. Hex. The Evil Eye.

A curse is something that happens to you, a streak of bad luck, a sort of supernatural force. Some people believe that humans can place a curse on a person they wish to harm. Others believe that a place can be cursed — simply going to that place will bring you bad luck. And others believe that objects themselves can carry powerful curses: To touch one of these objects may spell your doom.

Most say that cursing someone involves a ritual and removing a curse, a different ritual.

Some curses seem relatively silly and harmless, like when the Red Sox couldn't seem to win the World Series for all those years because of something that supposedly happened a long time ago to Babe Ruth. And yet other curses can kill you.

One of the most famous curse legends I've read about comes from Hawaii. It's the classic "don't take something from this place or you'll be sorry" hex, kind of like the ones with the mummies and the archaeologists and the pharaoh tombs in Egypt.

The story goes that in Hawaii, it's bad luck to remove lava rock from the island. That to do so makes the goddess Pele angry. If you're on vacation there and you take a rock home as a souvenir, all sorts of calamities will befall you. They say Pele can reach across the ocean and make you pay for taking what belongs to her. The only way to appease the goddess is to return the rock to the island from where you took it —

Chapter Thirty-Eight

CASSIDY STOPPED READING. "You guys, I think I found something."

The others had left her alone on the couch and had gathered around Hal's computer, presumably to look for the name of the company that had cleaned up Ursula's property. Ping glanced over her shoulder. "What is it, Cassidy?"

Cassidy stood, realizing that she was holding her book out in the open for everyone to see. She'd never shown it to anyone, not since Levi Stanton had given it to her. "I — I've got this notebook," she said. The boys turned to look at her too, obviously sensing something strange in her voice. "I collect information about . . . well, about bad things. And I remembered an entry I wrote about curses. I think you should hear it."

"Go on," said Joey.

Cassidy was surprised. She'd always assumed that people would make fun of her for it. But she shook off her surprise and read the entry aloud. "At this point," she added, "I think it's too late to get all the stuff back. The movers will only be more clueless and scared than we are. So instead of searching for the guys who emptied out Ursula's house, we need to look up everything we can about curses. And how to break them."

Hal wiped sweat from his top lip. "I think that's a great idea."

Cassidy slipped her notebook back into her bag, then joined the group at the computer desk by the window. "We might have to dig deeper than Wikipedia, but I'm not sure how."

"I bet there's a lot to read about curses in my magazines back home," said Ping.

At the computer, Hal opened the browser and began to type something into a search engine. "Let me try."

From the corner of her eye, Cassidy saw movement outside, in the Nances' backyard. At first, she thought nothing of it. Branches swaying in the hot breeze. But after a moment, something clicked, told her to turn, to look closer.

Owen Chase was coming through the woods toward the house, stumbling stiffly along, his face pale and bloated, pulling branches and vines roughly out of his way. He was trailed by several tall shadowy figures and a smaller, dog-shaped one, all moving in a similar fashion, rigid, jerking, stuttered, but determined.

CHAPTER THIRTY-NINE

CASSIDY CRIED OUT. The group jumped. She pointed at the glass. "They followed us!"

"Who followed us?" Joey shrieked.

"Followed us from where?" Hal whispered.

"Whoa," Ping said. The group gathered beside her at the window. For several seconds, they stared in silent horror, watching as the pale things that had chased them up Ursula's basement stairs pushed through the last barrier of brush and shadow and stepped onto the Nances' patchy lawn.

A humming sound vibrated the air. It tingled Cassidy's skin, tried to lull her heartbeat. In her head, she heard a deep voice whispering a slow chant. If it had been words, it would have sounded something like *Wait ... Wait ... Wait ...*

Five dead creatures paused and stared up at the house, as if they understood they were being observed. Lucky hung back in the shadows, but Owen Chase, in a shredded black suit and tie, stood beside his mother-in-law, Millie Moriarty, who wore a light-blue floral dress and one purple high-heeled shoe. Her other foot was bare. Her knobby toes had been painted pink. Each figure was dressed in what must have been their finest clothing — whatever their families had decided to bury them in.

Another man, if one could call him that, wavered on sticklike legs beside Millie. His clothes once may have been a nice shirt and pair of slacks but, after years in the dark underground, had become rags. His exposed skin was shriveled, vacuum-sealed to his bones.

His jaw hung open, his lips pulled back to expose what were left of his brown teeth. His hair was long and gray and wet, plastered to his skull and neck, dangling down to his shoulders. As Ursula Chambers stumbled onto the grass beside him, wearing her burgundy funeral gown, Cassidy whispered, "It's Aidan. Ursula's uncle. He's been down there with them too. Probably ever since he died. The house . . . No . . . The thing in the house, *the vortex-thing*, brought him back. That's why he looks so . . ."

"Dead," Joey whispered, his voice toneless, empty.

"Dead-*alive*," said Hal.

"*That* Ursula is not the Ursula from my dream last night," said Cassidy. "She's not the Ursula who's been warning people to return the things they took. This is the Ursula who belongs to the house."

"Why are they here?" Ping asked.

"Why do you think?" Joey said.

Ping swallowed — an audible gulp. No answer required. She stepped away from the window, pulling Cassidy and the others back as well.

"Obviously they know where we are," said Hal. "The house, or the thing in the house, sent them." He sniffed. "They're its sentinels. Its guardians."

"Why would the house need guardians?" said Ping. "Unless it thinks of us as a threat?"

"It might." Hal bit his lip. "Or maybe it just wants to own *us* too. They're here to make sure that happens."

"We have to go," Cassidy interrupted, waving the group toward the foyer.

"Where to?" Joey asked. "They'll find us. You know they will."

"My car's gone," said Hal. "Obviously."

"Then maybe we should stay put," said Ping.

"We don't have time to argue," Joey said, pushing past Cassidy to the front door. "They're out there." He pointed to the back of the house. He turned the knob, and the door opened a crack. "And they'll want to get in here. So that means we leave now. Walk, run, *unicycle*, I don't care. We just —"

Ping screamed as a large, furry shape leapt upon Joey, shoving him backward into the Nances' foyer.

CHAPTER FORTY

THE DOG'S GROWLS ECHOED off the high ceiling and mixed with the commotion of their panicked voices. It had pinned Joey to the floor. Once, a couple years ago, Cassidy had witnessed a similar scene, one in which Lucky's kisses left Joey's face covered in slobber and everyone involved was laughing. Now, Cassidy watched white teeth descend on her friend, the dog's jaw opened wider than seemed possible, its black lips raised in a snarl.

Without thinking, Cassidy smashed its exposed torso with her backpack, knocking the creature off balance. Joey curled into a ball. For a moment, she felt nauseated. This thing used to be her friend's pet.

It shook its large head. Its fur was matted with dirt and dried blood, and it stank like a festering wound. Its cloudy eyes locked onto her own, then it leapt at her. Cassidy threw herself to the side. What used to be Lucky collided with the wall behind her, leaving a large dent in the plaster, before tumbling to the tiled floor.

"Go!" she screamed. "All of you! Run!"

Ping and Hal grabbed Joey under their arms, lifting him to his feet, then dragged him quickly out the front door. Cassidy was on their heels as she heard the dog's claws scrabbling against the floor behind her. She didn't look back as she pulled the door shut. A second later, the door quaked. The group scrambled down the front steps.

The dog howled from just inside, a sound unlike anything any of them had ever heard. It seemed to rattle the ground, the grass, the molecules of the air. For a moment, Cassidy was certain that it was not the dog that they were hearing, but something else. Something deep in the ground at the top of the hill — that intelligent *something* that Hal had mentioned earlier.

Ping didn't wait for the sound to stop before lifting Joey's head to examine his face and neck. "Did he bite you?"

"I — I don't think so," said Joey. He brought up his hands, covered his face. His shoulders hitched. It took the others a moment to understand that he was crying, and only a moment after that, he forced himself to stop, wiping ferociously at his suddenly hard-set eyes. Cassidy thought she heard him mumble "Lucky," quickly, quietly, the way you say "Amen" at the end of a prayer when you have nothing left to say, when it's all over.

But it wasn't over.

The dead clamored through several squat holly bushes at the corner of the Nances' house, tearing through the shrubbery, their arms outstretched, their mouths open in silent stupor.

CHAPTER FORTY-ONE

CASSIDY RAN TOWARD THE STREET and didn't look back. The lawn was soft beneath her sneakers. She wished it were snarled with rocks and vines so that the creatures pursuing her might trip and fall.

The group dashed out into the middle of the intersection where Hal's street met Joey's. To their surprise, Ping's mother was in her minivan, slowing at the stop sign on the corner. When she spotted them, Mrs. Yu's mouth dropped open, and she slammed on the brakes.

"Come on." Ping waved the others forward, barreling toward her mother.

Mrs. Yu watched in astonishment as her daughter and her friends, along with a beat-up teenager, piled into her vehicle.

"Drive, Mom! Drive!" Ping screamed, leaning forward, peering down the street from which they'd come. It now appeared to be empty, as if the dead had hidden themselves in the holly.

"Okay! Okay!" shouted Ping's mother, signaling to the right and slowly pressing her foot against the gas pedal. "Calm down!" She turned onto Hal's street and eased toward the main gate. "What is wrong with you?"

"Nothing," Ping said, panting. The others sat in the backseat, their faces pressed against the windows. "Nothing wrong. We just wanted to see you."

"Really. *You wanted to see me.*" Mrs. Yu sighed, as if this were all part of a normal day. "Well, here I am. I'm heading to a meeting at the college. I'll let you off on the corner."

"No!" Cassidy, Joey, and Hal shouted at once. Mrs. Yu swerved the wheel as she passed by Hal's house.

She started to pull over. From the backseat, Cassidy read the gauge. Mrs. Yu was driving under five miles per hour. "You guys, I cannot —"

"Take us with you," Ping said, purposely calming her tone. She glanced in the rearview mirror at the side of the car. "We'll leave you alone. Hang out on the quad." She lowered her voice. "I promised them," she said, in a please-don't-embarrass-me manner.

"Oh, so you promised them," Mrs. Yu said sarcastically. She stopped the car entirely, shifting into park. "Well, next time, you might want to check with me first, young lady. And also? Not a good idea to leap out in front of cars in the middle of intersections. Are you trying to get yourselves killed?"

"We didn't want to miss you!" Ping tried.

"I almost didn't miss *you!*"

Cassidy turned around and peered out the back window. The dead were hiding. She imagined them crouched in the bushes or waiting just around the corner of the house. Jaws hanging askew. Black liquid dripping from swollen tongues. Cassidy turned back to Mrs. Yu. What would happen if she told her what was going on? Would Mrs. Yu get out of the car? Go searching for the creatures? And if she found them, what then?

"We're really sorry," Cassidy said, trying to control the tremor in her voice. "It's just, you know, I'm only visiting from the city for a short while. So Ping thought it would be fun for me to see where the big kids go to school. Something to look forward to." She blinked. What if the dead suddenly sprang out and rushed the car, pounding and scratching against the windows with clammy hands? Then Mrs. Yu would have no doubt. They'd drive off to safety, but soon the adults would enter the Chambers house to search for a solution. And the curse would spread even further. "But never mind. It's okay. We'll just get out here." Cassidy forced herself still to keep from shaking. She sensed that the others were trying to do the same.

Mrs. Yu checked the time in the dashboard. Then she knocked the gear back into drive. "Darn it, I'm late already." She yanked the wheel and pressed the gas, hard this time, making the last turn onto the main road out of the Estates. "But promise you'll never pull this stunt again." Mrs. Yu glared at Ping. "You'll be sorry if you do."

"I promise," Ping mumbled. She fastened her seat belt, then slumped down in the front seat, hugging her arms across her chest. Cassidy, Joey, and Hal simply stared at one another in the back-seat, unable to express the horror that raced through their minds and stopped on the tips of their tongues.

CHAPTER FORTY-TWO

THEY RODE THE REST of the way listening to the hum of the AC.

Cassidy remembered the drive from earlier in the week, when she and Joey went to the art class. It was like a lifetime ago.

She had a hunch that nothing would stop the dead from tracking them all the way here, but the length of the journey would buy them some time.

On the college campus, Mrs. Yu parked the car in a crowded lot. She led them to the stone building in which her office was located, then pointed them toward a large patch of grass that lay in the center of the many other campus structures. "There you go," she said. "The quad. Now, I'm going to be here for several hours. So if you get bored . . . too bad! I don't want to be bothered, got it?"

Ping nodded. "Got it," she chirped, smiling a bright smile.

Mrs. Yu hiked her heavy satchel onto her shoulder. Cassidy considered her own bag and the book she always kept inside. Glancing at it, she noticed clumps of dog hair clinging to its front. Disgusted, she brushed them off. Somehow, she'd remembered to grab it in the mad dash to leave the Nances' place. "But if you do need anything, security is located right over there. Emergencies only." Then she turned and headed up the stairs into the massive edifice.

The four made their way to the large lawn and plopped themselves down in the shade of a young elm. Each of them continuously glanced around into the shadows between buildings, looking for the shambling movement of the things that had nearly attacked them, impossible as it seemed.

"That dog is in my house," Hal whispered, pulling out his phone. "I have to warn my parents."

"Maybe one of the others let him out," said Ping. As Hal typed a text, she added, "Careful what you tell them."

"I'll keep it vague."

"It's *us* I'm worried about," said Joey. "Where are we gonna go?"

"My thoughts exactly," said Cassidy. "Maybe if we found our way back to the city —"

"Eventually, they'd find their way too," Ping insisted. "We have to do something to *stop them now*."

Joey pulled distractedly at his sneakers' laces. "In movies, you kill zombies with a blow to the head. Destroy the brain. We need to find a baseball bat. A hammer."

"You think you're capable of doing something like that?" Ping asked, lowering her voice.

"I think I'm capable of lots of things now. I'll do what I need to do to get us out of this mess."

"It wasn't zombies that caused my car accident," said Hal. "And I'm pretty sure it wasn't zombies that got to Mr. Chase or Mrs. Moriarty. It was something else. Something that lives in that house. Or underneath it."

"Inside the vortex," Ping said.

"None of that makes sense to me," said Joey.

"But it's all happening," Cassidy said. "If we're going to believe that one of these things is true, we have to open ourselves to the possibility that anything could be true."

Joey released a loud sigh. He squeezed his eyes shut and pulled at his shirt collar, stretching out the cotton. Finally he said, "So what do you think lives in that house, Hal? What is inside the vortex?"

"I'm not sure. But when I remember last night, I can't stop thinking about the humming sound I heard."

Cassidy chimed in. "I've heard the humming too! It woke me up the night I saw Ursula out in the street."

Hal nodded. "It felt almost as if something was digging around in my head. Like it was speaking, but without words. It felt like it was telling me what I was seeing. And what I saw was that mannequin grow a head and arms and claws. I can't explain it. I don't know if what I saw was real, but I *believed* it was real. And that's what made it dangerous. If Ping's right, then whatever is living inside the vortex *is* intelligent. And its reach is far. And terrifying."

"Can it get at us all the way out here?" Cassidy asked, tearing up clumps of grass. She didn't want to say that she could feel it watching, listening, investigating the veil of reality to find a loosened thread through which it might sneak. What worried her the most was the feeling that the loose thread may be in her head, in each of their heads, and one errant thought, one wrong word would give it access to their most precious possessions. Their *selves*.

"I wouldn't be surprised if it tried," said Hal.

"Like I said," Ping piped up, "we have to fight."

"Fight?" Joey asked. "How? With what? Hal says killing our zombie friends won't stop what's happening in this town. Or to us. Right? The thing in that house thinks it owns us now. Just like it owns Ursula and the others. And Lucky." He blinked, momentarily retreating into his head. "How do we change that?"

"The library?" Ping suggested, nodding at a wide brick building that stood on the opposite side of the quad. "If we're gonna find the answer before my mom shows up to take us home, we've gotta look there."

CHAPTER FORTY-THREE

THE LIBRARY WAS COLD AND DARK. Beyond the front desk, rows of tables filled a long room. Dozens of small lamps sat on the tables. A dim glow filled the space. Bookshelves lined the walls. Ladders were propped up in several spots so that anyone could reach the highest books.

"Are you kids students?" said the man behind the desk. He wore a jean vest and a gray T-shirt. His pitch-black hair was tied back in a ponytail. His tired eyes were saddled with puffy, slightly wrinkled bags. Cassidy thought he looked more like a member of a biker gang than a librarian; then again, she'd lately seen stranger things than this. Beside his desk stood a glass barrier and a rotary turnstile, like the ones in the city subway stations.

"My mom's a professor here," said Ping. "We need to use the library."

"Is your mom with you?" he said, sizing them up. He stared especially long at Hal, whose bruises and bloodied eyeball must have set off all kinds of alarms.

"She's in a meeting."

"Well, when she gets out, have her meet you here. Then I can sign you all in."

"This is kind of an emergency," Ping whispered.

"An emergency?" said the man. "Wow. This sounds exciting." He leaned forward, as if he expected to hear a story of action and adventure. It took Cassidy a few seconds to register his sarcasm. He tapped the desk with a pencil. "Sorry, kids. I really can't let just anyone through the gate. What if one of you turned out to be some sort of dangerous criminal? Someone has to be held responsible. You want me to lose my job if one of you goes off the deep end?"

Cassidy watched as Joey squeezed his hands into fists. The guy behind the desk had no idea how close he was to being right. "People are dying," Joey whispered. Cassidy felt her cheeks burn. The man squinted at them, as if he hadn't heard correctly. Several patrons passed his desk showing their IDs, unaware of the little drama playing out only a few feet away. "You said someone has to be held responsible? Well, if you don't let us in here, you'll be responsible for what happens to this town. How about that?" Cassidy wanted to grab his hand and raise it like a boxer who'd just won a fight. Yes. This was the Joey she remembered.

Wide-eyed, the man reached for a phone sitting next to his computer. "How about this," he said, "you guys all turn around and walk out of here right now, and I won't call security?"

Ping shot Joey a look of death. Hal swayed, looking ready to walk out the door. But Cassidy stared into the library, seeing what she hoped might be the key to their entry past the gatekeeper. Sitting at the table closest to the front, a young man flipped through an oversized art book.

"Vic!" Cassidy called out. Her voice echoed through the otherwise quiet chamber. When the art teacher glanced up, she waved her arms over her head like someone who was drowning.

CHAPTER FORTY-FOUR

VIC APPROACHED THE FRONT DESK, standing beyond the turnstile. "Hey there! You guys coming back to my class next Tuesday?"

"We hope so," said Cassidy, glancing at Joey, who looked mortified.

"Cool," said Vic. "That would be fantastic. We're going to be working on —"

"Excuse me," said the desk attendant. "What the heck is going on here?"

Cassidy ignored him. "We need to use the library. But he won't let us through."

"Really? Why not?" Vic crossed his arms, smiling a confused and charming smile.

The biker-librarian was flustered. "They're not students. They're not guests."

"These two are my students," said Vic, winking at Cassidy. "The others, well, they can be my guests. Can't you let them through?"

The man sighed, defeated. "Sign 'em in," he said, handing Vic a ledger and a pen.

Afterward, Vic waved them all forward. One by one, they passed through the turnstile. Joey leaned toward the desk and whispered, "You won't regret this."

Ping smiled and said thank you, then quickly pulled Joey away from the entry before the man could change his mind. Cassidy followed. Nearly everyone sitting in the main room watched them

enter. As long as every pair of eyes stared out from a living, breathing human, she didn't even care.

When they reached the table where Vic had been working, he
lost his smile. "So what are you guys doing here?" he asked, his
tone now serious. "That was bad form back there. I really can't get
kicked out of the library this afternoon." He glared at Joey and
Cassidy. "You gonna pull another stunt like the one you tried on
Tuesday?"

"No," they answered, sounding like scolded children, which
Cassidy realized, they sort of were.

"Good. I want you guys in my class. But I want you to *want* to
be there too."

"We do," said Cassidy. "You have no idea how badly we want
to be there next week."

"No idea," Joey mumbled.

"Ping wasn't lying. Her mom is a professor here," Cassidy
explained. "We need to do some research, but that guy wouldn't let
us in without her."

"But there's a public library in Whitechapel," said Vic. "And
don't tell me you have no Internet at home."

"We can't really be at home right now," Joey said. Vic squinted,
as if putting together puzzle pieces in his mind. "Thank you for
helping us. We'll behave. Promise."

Vic sighed. "Fine." He sat down, opening the large book on
the table. "Go forth, then. Research and be well. Hope you find
what you're looking for."

CASSIDY'S BOOK OF BAD THINGS, ENTRY #2:
PANIC ATTACKS

They say the world can be a scary place. I totally agree. But when you have a panic attack, the world becomes much scarier than usual.

My guidance counselor, Mrs. Ames, told me today that she thinks I've been suffering from panic attacks. According to her, lots of people deal with them. She promised me that I'm not going crazy. Which was a relief. Sort of.

Mrs. Ames explained that there is this chemical my brain makes when I get scared. It's called adrenaline. She said normally, when adrenaline rushes into our veins, people have a reaction to it that she called "fight or flight." This means either you stand your ground or you run away.

But with me, she said, the adrenaline-stuff just keeps coming and coming. I become sort of paralyzed. I get dizzy and I can't breathe. I can't fight <u>or</u> flight.

The scariest part is how everything around me feels really strange. Like REALLY strange. And it's this part of it that made me worry my brain was broken.

Like, the first time it happened, I was sitting in music class and a dump truck passed by outside. It hit the road and bounced and made this really loud clanging sound. And all of a sudden, I couldn't hear the words Mrs. Mendez was saying. I only heard her voice, which had twisted up into this weird high-pitched squeal.

When I glanced around to see if any of my classmates noticed, I realized most of them were staring at me. They all looked really angry with me. Almost hungry too. As if they were wild dogs and I was a juicy steak.

That's when I realized I couldn't catch my breath. I felt like I was going to puke.

I stood up and backed against the wall, certain that everyone was about to chase after me. And if they caught me...I don't know what.

Eventually, Mrs. Mendez took me to the nurse's office where they made me lay down on a cot and drink some water.

Since then, the attacks mostly come when I'm home alone. At night. I hear slithering noises in the hall. I see movement in the shadows of the living room.

I know that Mr. Stanton is next door, and he said I could knock whenever I need to. I just wish I didn't need to.

Mrs. Ames said that there are ways to beat the attacks, but that it takes work. She explained that whenever I feel one coming on, I must remember that it's only temporary. But when your mind is trying to freak you out, it's hard to remember anything. And the last thing you want to do at that point is work. The only thing you want to do is curl into a ball so small that you disappear.

CHAPTER FORTY-FIVE

CASSIDY, JOEY, PING, AND HAL found a bank of computers in the center of the room. They pulled up the library catalogue. Ping entered some keywords into the search field — ley lines, vortexes, curses — and soon the group had acquired a short list of books and periodicals that they thought might provide answers to their questions. Ping printed out the results for each of them. To save time, they decided to split up.

Cassidy clutched her paper in one hand and a strap of her backpack in the other. The library was immense, the dark ceiling as high as a cathedral's. From the front of the space to the back, a dozen aisles led off into the stacks, many of them disappearing into shadow. Dewey decimal system numbers were posted at each corridor, labeled by category, white on black. Cassidy checked the digits on her list and headed purposefully toward the first corresponding aisle.

Out of the corner of her eye, she watched the others spread out, vanishing into their own corridors. The farther away from the main space she strolled, the faster Cassidy's heart raced. She suddenly felt very alone. And very afraid. She was tempted to go back and chase after Ping. Why hadn't they partnered up?

What would she do if she came around a dark corner to find the gaping mouth of Owen Chase waiting for her?

Where was this stupid book?

Cassidy scanned the shelves for the title. *Archaeology and Folklore of the Twentieth Century. Sounds snooze-tastic,* Cassidy thought, trying to make herself laugh. It didn't work. The prospect of flipping through hundreds of pages to find an answer filled her with a sense of dread, which only grew larger when the fluorescent lights over her head began to flicker.

She held her breath, froze all movement.

The lights sputtered, then quickly faded away. Instinctively, Cassidy reached her arms out, gripping opposite shelves. She pressed her lips together. Light from the main room spilled about halfway down the aisle, and an ambient glow came through the spaces between books from the passages on either side of her.

Cassidy stood still, keeping her mind quiet. She would not run away like she had that awful night in New York. Not this time. That was what the vortex-thing would want her to do. She was nobody's puppet. Mr. Stanton had taught her that years ago.

Listening to the sound of her own breath, she studied the dim titles of the books surrounding her. *It must be here, somewhere,* she thought, fighting against the dark images her brain was producing. Pushing it all away, she ran her fingers along the spines, squinting to read the words through the blanket of encroaching shadow. "Wh-where *are* you?" she stammered.

The floor shuddered. The books trembled. Cassidy thought of the subway at night, passing through her neighborhood. She pulled back, glancing all around. Down the aisle, in the light, people were moving around the main room. No one else seemed to notice the disturbance.

A low growl filled the air, barely audible. The sound vibrated in her stomach, and she recognized it. That familiar humming. The vortex-thing was here. It had found her. Her confidence began to ebb. Cassidy knew if she moved at all now, she'd collapse, or wet herself, or something worse, so she planted her feet. She closed her eyes, and a dizzying flood of strange images spun past the inside of her eyelids — objects she recognized from Ursula's driveway, in the Dumpsters, scattered on the ground.

Her spine smacked the shelves behind her; she felt faint. When she opened her eyes again, through the space between books, she saw an enormous shadowy shape moving, no, *pulsing* down the next aisle, like a giant black worm, into the darkness away from the main room. As it slid past her, she noticed iridescent scales glistening on its back. She opened her mouth to scream, but all that came out was a silent puff of air.

An angry voice whispered, maybe in her head, maybe aloud, *Bring it back . . . Bring it back . . . Bring it back to me . . .*

Chapter Forty-Six

A BOOK FELL TO THE GROUND with a resounding *whap*, jarring Cassidy away from the horrible vision in the adjacent aisle.

She blinked, and the creature was gone. Only the echo of its voice remained.

Bring . . . it . . . back . . .

Cassidy exhaled, feeling her shoulders relax slightly now that the beast had disappeared. Glancing at the floor, she saw a vague impression of a title staring up at her. *Archaeology and Folklore of the Twentieth Century.*

As she bent to pick it up, she saw a pair of feet slide into the shadow at her left. She grabbed the book and stood, easing away from whoever was still in the aisle with her. At this point, Cassidy didn't care how foolish she looked dashing out into the main room like a girl gone mad. But when she recognized the person who had knocked the book to the floor, she stopped and stared in awe.

Ursula was only there for a moment longer, dressed in her colorless jogging suit like the one she'd worn in Cassidy's dream. A kind and sad smile decorated her face, before she disappeared into the reaches of the dim corridor.

Cassidy found her way back to the corner where the group had agreed to meet. From the looks on Ping's and Joey's faces, she hadn't been the only one who had been visited by the beast. A pile of books lay on the table between them.

When Hal arrived moments later, Cassidy told them all what she'd seen and heard. Ping and Joey shared their own stories, which were almost exactly the same as Cassidy's. The flickering lights. The humming. The black, snaky worm-thing. The whispering voice.

Hal listened in awe. While looking for the books on his short list, he hadn't experienced anything of the sort. He wondered aloud if it was because he'd returned the mannequin that morning.

"It's the thing from the vortex," said Joey. "The beast found us. It's gonna send the dead to get us."

"It said 'Bring it back,'" Cassidy mentioned. "But what? We didn't take anything from the house."

"Maybe it's not talking about an object," said Ping. "Maybe it's talking about *us*."

"Us?" said Cassidy. "What do you mean, *us*?"

"We went into the house. We spent some time standing at the vortex. In the vortex. Maybe what Joey said before is right — this creature thinks it owns us now. We're the *it* that it's talking about."

Cassidy shivered. "What if the creature comes back? What if it tries to take us?"

"If we're not safe now," said Hal, "we're never going to be safe."

"But you're safe, Hal. Aren't you?" Joey asked. "You didn't see what we saw."

"I don't feel safe."

"I'm not sure it was even here in the first place," said Ping. "The other night, it sent a vision to Hal. Today, we all shared a vision too, like a daydream. I think it's only reaching out. Searching for us."

"And if you don't return to the house," said Hal, "it will find a way to bring you back there. Trust me. I've seen what it can do."

"Ursula was trapped in that house," said Cassidy. "If we go back, we might be trapped too."

"With a bunch of zombies, apparently," said Joey.

"Are we willing to risk that?" Hal asked. "Being trapped in order to save our friends? Our families?" The group was quiet for a moment, considering Hal's question. "I mean, Ursula wasn't really a hoarder at all, was she? She gave up everything that mattered, everything she cared about, even her reputation, her dignity, to protect people."

Cassidy thought of Mr. Faros and the lesson about Theseus and the Minotaur. Theseus had chosen to enter the Cretan labyrinth in order to stop King Minos from sacrificing any more young people to the monster. Was Ursula — an eccentric and frail old woman — like Theseus? A true hero? If so, was it possible for Cassidy to be the same?

She understood that they had two options: fight or flight. Both seemed equally as dangerous. Fight and they may succumb to the monster. Flee and the monster would continue to pursue them. But if they stood their ground, at least they had a chance of winning, however small. "*I'm* willing to risk that," Cassidy said, surprising herself. Her friends heard her, and after a moment, each of them nodded tentatively.

"We should all stay together from now on," Ping suggested, pulling out a chair and finally sitting down. "I think the . . . *beast* was able to get into our heads because we went off by ourselves. Maybe it can only reach out to us when we're alone."

"Fine," said Cassidy, also sitting down. "Then let's do what we came here to do." She grabbed the book that had minutes earlier caused her so much trouble and opened to the table of contents. "Together."

CHAPTER FORTY-SEVEN

EVERY LITTLE NOISE THAT echoed through the great space caused everyone at the small table to jump. Now and again, they interrupted their research by reading aloud bits of information that they'd discovered.

One article that Joey found discussed the history of ley lines in England and made a comparison to some long forgotten roads in Vermont.

Cassidy discovered some information about vortexes out in the Southwest, how these particular spots supposedly had healing properties, physical and mental, and that people made pilgrimages to visit these locations.

"I can't imagine anyone wanting to visit our special little spot here in New Jersey," said Joey. "Not for *healing* anyway."

Hal read to them from a book about folklore, about how immigrants to North America had brought with them stories of gods and goddesses from the old countries. The author of the book surmised that when some of these old stories had been lost over generations, new gods had sprung up to take their place. "I guess it makes sense," he said, looking up from the passage. "If we're dealing with some sort of entity that exists on this continent, like a new god . . . or a new devil . . . it would be one that reveres *owning* things. A new religion: selfishness."

"New god. Old devil," said Joey. "I just want it to leave us alone. Hasn't anyone found something that can help us?"

Ping gave a small wave. "I think I might have something here." She scanned the open book in front of her, swiftly moving her index finger along the page. "I was just looking at a chapter about other dimensions. Wormholes. Portals. Vortexes. It says that ancient cultures knew of special spots, *convergences* it says here, and they often marked them with stone. As a sacred act. All over the world, people have built pyramids, circles of rocks, *henges*."

"So all we need to do is build a pyramid?" Joey asked, his eyebrow raised.

"No," said Ping, flustered. She frowned at the page, as if her answer were written in the space between the words. "It wasn't about what the people built there. What helped them was the *idea* of protecting themselves from big bad things. Things beyond their comprehension. This book says that some people believed that it wasn't the *huge* efforts of the civilization that did the trick — you know, the pyramids, the circles — but the smaller attempts of the local people, like old rituals and prayers, that acted as a seal of protection against evil."

"A seal of protection?" Cassidy asked. "That sounds like our answer!"

"I don't know what that means," said Joey. "What kind of *small attempt* can we make? I don't know any old prayers."

Ping flipped through the next several pages. Her eyes grew wide. "Wow. I think I might have found an answer." She glanced up from the book. "There's a supposedly true account here of a place in England, a village called Gingerwich that sat on top of one of the ancient ley lines. Listen to this."

And Ping told them a story.

THE GINGERWICH CURSE

In a grassy field located several hundred kilometers north of Stonehenge's Salisbury Plain, just outside the village of Gingerwich, a druidic stone circle stands: a site that archeologists claim dates back even further than the most famous of British henges by at least a century.

The Gingerwich circle is wider in diameter than Stonehenge by about twelve meters. However, its design is simpler. Originally made of thirteen bluestone monoliths, each weighing at least a ton and standing two to three meters tall, the pieces were arranged in a circular formation with none of the embellishments of its southern neighbor's inner rings and horseshoe formations.

In the mid-twentieth century, after the discovery of cremated human remains, archeologists theorized that the circle had been created as a burial site and that, several millennia earlier, it had been considered a holy place. Unfortunately, the people who lived in the area in the late eighteenth and early nineteenth centuries were unaware of these burials.

The village of Gingerwich, its houses and barns built originally from locally forested wood, had existed for centuries near the monoliths; however, as the population began to grow, one of its more inventive citizens decided that the village's older structures may benefit from reinforcement — the closest resource being the abundant bluestone monoliths in the nearby fields.

Local masons broke pieces from the stones, and in at least three cases, destroyed the monoliths almost entirely to their bases.

Using these pieces, they added decorations to their homes. They also constructed new houses and barns.

Some of the population warned that using the ancient stones in this manner would be a grave mistake. And soon, tales sprang up of a curse upon the structures built from the circle's broken stones.

There is evidence that the families who lived in the stone houses of Gingerwich befell early deaths from farming accidents and sickness. There are tales of failed crops, livestock deaths, still-births, even murder. Even more frightening tales exist: Rumors spread that dark figures roamed the village at night, sometimes entering houses to watch people asleep in their beds. Those who'd seen the creatures claimed that they walked upright like humans, but their bodies were goatlike and skeletal, with wide, twisted antlers rising from their skulls.

The structures that had been built using the stones were eventually abandoned, but the troubles did not end there. Bad luck continued to befall the people of Gingerwich. The more superstitious folk claimed that demons now haunted the area, taking revenge upon the descendants of folk who had disrespected the stone circle.

Legend tells that near the turn of the twentieth century a group of citizens banded together, determined to stop the curse that had wreaked havoc upon their ancestors. They believed that simply dismantling the abandoned houses would have no effect on the curse or the demons; the damage to the monoliths, after all, could not be repaired. Instead, it was decided that they would need to look into their pre-Christian history for something to appease these pre-Christian spirits.

Collecting the few precious metals they owned, the people melted down their fortunes and forged a piece of jewelry. Its design was based upon the ancient pagan symbol for protection: a simple pentacle, the five points of which touched upon an unbroken circle. It was as close a reparation for the ruined circle at the town's edge as they could imagine.

Believing that the offering would stop the demons' wrath, the group entered one of the stone houses, searching the basement for what they believed was the heart of the house. In the darkness underground, they discovered an entry to a system of caves. Armed with torches, they made their way deep inside the twisting caverns, journeying until they could go no farther. It was there that they left their offering.

After the group returned to the surface, life soon returned to normalcy. It was determined that the pentacle had ended the curse.

The village of Gingerwich still stands today. The stone houses, however, have finally been disassembled, their pieces scattered across the nearby countryside, lost to the vagaries of nature and time and whatever gods or demons still hold sway over them.

CHAPTER FORTY-EIGHT

"THAT IS REALLY FREAKY," said Joey.

"No freakier than what we're dealing with right here in Whitechapel," said Hal.

"What if we make an offering like the people of Gingerwich did?" asked Cassidy.

"Yeah, like a *present*," said Ping. "Our little beastie seems to crave presents, right? We just need to find him the right one."

"A KEEP OUT sign?" Joey said.

"Well, no. Not quite. It has to have meaning."

Cassidy lit up. "Today we found stars carved into Ursula's floor. The people in Gingerwich offered up a pentacle. That can't be a coincidence, can it? Would it make sense for us to do the same thing?"

"I think you're right," said Ping. "Something with a star symbol on it. Something *old*. An artifact. A pendant. A drawing. A sculpture."

"And then?" said Joey. "We bring our *star* back to the house and leave it there? Like how Hal left his mannequin in the foyer?"

Ping grimaced, then shuddered. "That's not how they did it in Gingerwich."

"What are you suggesting?" said Hal.

"Even if we find what we're looking for, bringing the present into *the house* isn't going to be enough. But there's a crevice in the wall of Ursula's cellar. Strange how such a huge crack would appear in a recent concrete foundation, right? If our own experience sort of mirrors what happened in Gingerwich, the crack in the wall might lead to a tunnel or cavern. If so, I'll bet that's where *our* demon is hiding.

Cassidy nodded. "We'll bring him his gift — *the seal of protection* — and give it to him ourselves."

"That's crazy," said Joey. Everyone at the table stared at him. "We already know what's down in that basement. The dead crawled out of that crevice you're talking about. If we go in there, we might never make it back out."

"So we do nothing?" Cassidy asked. "Scary things are coming for us. Joey, we can't just go hide in your bedroom closet. Either we do this . . . or we die."

Joey shoved his pinky finger into his mouth and chewed at it. After a few seconds, Cassidy's words seemed to sink in, and he spit out a mangled piece of his fingernail onto the floor. Everyone else groaned. "So we need a star. An artifact." He glanced at Ping. "Where do we start?"

"We *are* on a college campus. There's got to be some sort of special collection in one of these big buildings. Anthropology? Archaeology? I'm sure there are rooms *filled* with stuff we could use."

Hal sniffed. "And you think it's going to be any easier getting into those places than it was getting into the library? I don't know about you guys, but I've never participated in a heist before."

"But there's another place nearby that might also have what we need," said Cassidy. She picked up her bag from the floor and laid it on the table. From inside one of its smaller, hidden compartments she pulled out a pink crystal elephant, the one she'd named Triumphant.

Outside, the afternoon sun glared down. They had to hurry. If the dead were scary in full sunlight, Cassidy didn't wish to imagine their faces after nightfall.

As the group crossed the quad, Ping told them her new plan. She'd head into the building where her mother's office was. The security guards knew her there, so they wouldn't question her when she went through. If her mother was still at her meeting, it was possible that her pocketbook was inside her office. Ping would *borrow* the car keys.

"Hopefully we can make it to Junkland and back before she even realizes we're gone."

"This feels wrong," said Hal, as they stopped in front of the building. "Like stealing."

"We don't have a choice," said Ping. "She's not going to drive us there. Especially not if we tell her the reason we need to go. We can't walk. What if we run into our *friends* on the road? What other options do we have?"

Though it wasn't ideal, they all agreed that Ping's plan would be the quickest and easiest way.

A few minutes later, they found themselves running toward the parking lot, the keys jangling from Ping's clutched fist. At the minivan, she tossed them to Hal, who suddenly looked frightened. He shook his head and whispered to himself, something that sounded like, "You can do this." Cassidy thought to herself that before the day was over, she would be telling herself the same thing. Hal unlocked the van, and they all climbed in.

Chapter Forty-Nine

When they arrived at the store, Cassidy was surprised to see that the sign over the front door read GRACELAND REFURBISHMENTS. She'd forgotten its actual name was not Junkland.

Behind the counter near the entrance, the two teenagers that had been there the other day dabbed at their foreheads with crumpled pieces of paper towel. The girl wore a ratty red T-shirt with a faded logo and a long, wrinkled skirt that looked like it had been made out of an Indian tapestry. Her hair was thick and red, divided into two messy braids that hung to her shoulders. Around her neck were dozens of thin chains and cords, beads and baubles. The boy beside her looked like he could be her brother; his own red hair was shoved up underneath a soggy-looking baseball cap. They waved hello apologetically. The air-conditioning was busted.

"Does anyone have any money?" Joey asked as the group moved down one aisle.

Hal pulled out a small wad of cash from his pocket. "Not much."

"We'll just have to be thrifty," said Ping, chipper as always.

Cassidy wondered how she managed to keep it up. "Can we stay together this time?" she asked. "I really don't want that *thing* to sneak up on me again." As if any of them did.

They wandered the store, fanning themselves uselessly against the stifling heat. Though she was starting to feel dizzy, Cassidy glanced at the bottom of every glass case and the top of every high shelf. Joey picked up a roll of stickers, star-shaped and glittery. "Does this count?" he asked, with a look that said he already knew the answer.

"Cassidy could put them in her notebook," said Hal with a smile. "But I doubt those are going to help us save the world."

Cassidy felt her face burn. "How'd you know about my . . ." she started to ask before remembering that she'd showed it to them back at Hal's house that morning. "Oh, right."

They continued their search as Ping asked, "What's with your notebook anyway? You said you collect information about *bad things*? Why?"

Cassidy felt her throat constrict. Darkness came at her from the corners of her vision. She clenched her fists and forced the anxiety away. Looking into Ping's eyes, she explained. "It's . . . for security," she said. The others stopped to listen. "A few years ago . . . something really scary happened to me." Pictures of that night flashed through her head. She slipped her bag off her shoulder, removed the notebook, then hugged it to her chest.

No one asked her what it was that had happened. They simply looked at her, giving her time to collect her thoughts, and if she felt the need, to put them into words. Cassidy knew if any of them had pressed her to continue, she wouldn't have been able to. But on her own terms, she flipped the book open to the first page and showed them what she'd written there.

Cassidy's Book of Bad Things, Entry #1: **Intruders**

CHAPTER FIFTY

"I WAS EIGHT YEARS OLD," Cassidy said. "Sometimes my mom, Naomi, worked late, and I had to stay home by myself. Usually, it was fine. I'd do my homework and watch television and fall asleep on the couch until she came home. Then she'd turn out the lights and pull the blanket over me and kiss me goodnight.

"I wasn't ever allowed in her bedroom. In fact, she kept the door padlocked. I never thought about why, but now I know. It was where she hid her *valuables*. I never found out what kind of *valuables* they were, but I figure if it was worth enough for a mother to lock them away from her own daughter, then maybe I was better off not knowing."

Cassidy sighed, remembering. It wasn't an easy thing to do. And saying the story out loud was even harder. Somehow though, suddenly choosing to reveal this secret to her three friends — who were listening as if their lives depended on it — seemed as important as locating the artifact for which they'd come searching.

"One night, I heard a noise," she went on. "It was way too early for my mom to be home. I jumped off the couch and ran to the bathroom just as the apartment door opened. Someone had come in. The only other person with a key was Naomi's boyfriend, Lou.

"Lou was never really nice to me. He always looked at me like I *knew* something, like I had X-ray vision. Like I could see inside his soul. And I guess I could, because I never trusted him, not for a moment.

"I heard him mumbling as he stumbled through the living room. He went for my mom's door, but he realized that none of the keys he had would open the padlock. He cursed. All sorts of nasty words. Then he started pounding on the door, then kicking until it just snapped off the hinges and leaned toward the floor. Then he kicked it some more.

"I didn't know what to do. I was sure that if he knew I was there, he'd hurt me. I held my breath, listening until he'd made his way into Naomi's room.

"I crept out into the living room, as quietly as I could. I could see his shadow against the wall in my mother's room. He was shouting, *Where is it? Where is it?*"

Bring it back to me, Cassidy thought, pausing, hearing the beast's voice in her head.

"He knocked over Naomi's bureau. The floor shook as it fell. I used the noise of his tantrum to mask the sound of my footsteps across the living room. Then, I ran into the hallway outside and knocked on the closest door, praying Lou wouldn't hear me. After a few seconds, this old man I'd never seen before answered. He had on a worn-out pair of khaki pants and a white tank top and he kind of smelled like . . . well, this store.

"I guess I looked like a time bomb about to explode, because he pulled me inside. At the time, I wasn't thinking how dangerous it was to go into a stranger's home. All I wanted was to get away from Lou. The old man held his finger up to his lips, as if he understood, as if he'd heard everything, then turned off the light on his desk a few feet away.

"His name was Levi Stanton. He didn't *live* in the building but only rented a small studio to use as an office. He was a writer . . . a crime novelist . . . a *famous* crime novelist, I found out afterward. The space was cheap, and my neighborhood was inspiring to him. But that night, he was the old man who tried to save me.

"We hid in the dark together, listening as Lou came barreling out of my apartment. He called out my name. He'd remembered

that I should have been home. His voice echoed through the hallways. We listened as Lou's footsteps came *calmly* down the corridor.
This frightened me more than his rage. I held my breath when he
stopped in front of us. I could see the shadows of his boots in the
space at the bottom of the door. He stood there for a few seconds,
then he whispered my name. The old man squeezed my hand and
I almost burst into tears. But then Lou just left. He strolled out of
the building and was gone."

CHAPTER FIFTY-ONE

THE ROOF CREAKED as a slight wind picked up outside the store.

Joey, Hal, and Ping stood before her, the four of them forming a small ring, as if they'd just finished some sort of sacred ritual. Cassidy let her arms fall to her sides, the notebook brushing her hip. She told them how Mr. Stanton called the police, then her mother at work, how there was an investigation, how they tracked down Lou. He was now in jail for several convictions — not only for the break-in, but for other, even scarier crimes.

"That's really . . ." Joey tried to respond. "How did you . . ." But the words wouldn't come.

"Survive?" Cassidy finished for him. She held up the book again. Waggled it a bit. "This." She walked, waving the group forward to continue their search as she talked. "After that night, I started feeling weird when I was at school. And when I came home, I would get sick. Dizzy. Pukey. Whenever I was able to fall asleep, my dreams were so freaky I thought I was going crazy. This started happening every day. My doctor wanted to give me medicine but Naomi said no, that I needed to stop being silly and just get over it."

"That's horrible," said Ping.

Cassidy blinked and rubbed at her nose. She'd never be able to explain her mother to anyone who didn't know her, so she'd stopped trying a long time ago. "Mr. Stanton checked in on me. Asked me how I was feeling. I told him. One day, he brought me this notebook. He told me to write down what scared me. He said putting it all on paper would help me sort it out in my head.

"I started with the night Lou broke in. And I haven't stopped since. For some reason, Mr. Stanton's advice worked. I guess putting my thoughts, my *fears* into sentences helps me find . . . *order* in the world. Which is kind of cool, because at least where I live, it feels like there's just so much . . . What's the word . . . Chaos?"

"This Levi Stanton guy sounds pretty awesome," said Hal. "If we get through this day, I'm gonna pick up some of his books."

If we get through this day . . . Hal's statement hung in the stagnant air, reminding them why they had come here and what might be waiting for them outside.

"Duh!" Ping threw her hands into the air. "Why don't we just ask the two at the front desk if they can help us?"

Back at the desk, Ping did the talking. She kept the story simple. "We need something old. Something star-shaped. Something . . . precious. You have anything like that?"

The girl at the register looked perplexed, rolling her eyes back into her head as if that's where she'd recorded all of the store's data. The boy beside her wiped at his forehead again. He stared intensely out into the aisles, as if he might spot what Ping had asked for.

"I don't think so," said the girl. "I'm sorry. I can take down your phone number. Give you guys a call if something comes in."

The boy's face lit up. He turned to the girl. "But something did come in," he said. "Just last week."

She looked perplexed. "Really? Where is it?"

The boy reached out and grasped at the tangle of chains around the girl's neck. She flinched. Then, with a groan, she allowed him to sort through the loops and ornaments. From the bottom of one cord, a charm glistened darkly. The boy managed to separate this necklace from the others, holding it away from the girl's skin so they could see it clearly.

A small pendant. A silver circle inside of which gleamed a shining pentacle. Just like in the Gingerwich story. *The seal of protection.*

"This what you're looking for?" the boy asked.

CHAPTER FIFTY-TWO

AFTER THE BOY WHISPERED some soft threats about "telling Mom," he managed to talk the girl into giving up the pendant and the chain. Hal gave them all his cash for it. Twelve dollars. "A real bargain," the girl said sarcastically as she slipped the pendant into a slim plastic Baggie. Hal handed it to Cassidy. She folded it into her notebook and stuck it deep into her backpack.

As the group passed through the exit, Cassidy overheard the redheaded siblings arguing, something about the group being the only customers all day and how any sale is a sale and how a sale is the most important thing. Cassidy wasn't sure she agreed with him, but for now, she was happy that the boy believed it.

A quick glance around the parking lot — no zombies, thank goodness. The group dashed for the minivan.

They made it to the college in no time, and Ping managed to sneak the keys back to her mother's office with a few minutes to spare.

Mrs. Yu found them sitting in the shadow of one of the quad's trees. She approached, shaking her head. "I'd think you all might have something better to do with your day than simply lounge around in the shade."

"Actually, we did spend some time at the library," said Ping matter-of-factly. "They've got a ton of really interesting books. Right, you guys?" The others nodded emphatically, forcing themselves to smile. They all looked a little crazy.

"We learned a whole lot," Joey concluded.

Minutes later, the group was back at the minivan. Cassidy

watched everyone else pile into the vehicle, but she couldn't bring herself to do the same. Standing on the steamy blacktop of the parking lot, way out here at the college, Cassidy felt like this was the last time she could ever be sure of herself, of her life. She tried to step forward but found she was frozen. Joey peered out the door of the van. He held out his hand to her. Cassidy stared at it, at the creases in his palm, the dirt and grime that had collected there over the course of the day. She thought of the story she'd shared with her friends back at Junkland — her darkest memory. She imagined the collection of bad things that she carried with her everywhere she went, how, over the years, with every entry, the notebook had continued to ease her mind. But the book couldn't help her now.

Bad things lived in the world.

She could continue to write them all down if she made it through this day, but for now, she had to move, to act, whether her brain wanted her to or not.

"Coming?" Joey asked, wiggling his fingers. His eyes were open, understanding, containing a kindness she hadn't seen in them for a long time. Cassidy reached out and took his hand.

CHAPTER FIFTY-THREE

DURING THE RIDE BACK to Chase Estates, Mrs. Yu occasionally glanced at them in the rearview mirror. They were all huddled together in the backseat, each lost in his or her own thoughts. Before the last turn, she offered to take them for ice cream. Without speaking, they peered at one another, then shook their heads.

"What's going on?" she asked Ping once she'd pulled into her driveway. "You're not telling me something." The others wandered around the lawn and waited for Ping to join them. They couldn't help but listen in. What would happen if Ping just told her mother everything? Cassidy tried to imagine the conversation: *We have to go fight some nameless evil thing that lives underneath the old house at the end of the road. . . .* But that was as far as Cassidy's mind allowed her to go. She knew that Mrs. Yu wouldn't hear the rest. Either she'd be angry or amused, then eventually, finally dismissive. This was one of the curses of being young: Adults rarely truly hear you, and when they did, they usually asked you why you didn't speak up sooner.

"We're just doing some research about the history of this land. About what was here before these houses or the Chambers farm."

Mrs. Yu squinted at Ping. "Why?"

"Why not?"

Somehow, this struck Mrs. Yu as a valid answer. "But why is that older boy tagging along? Doesn't he have friends his own age?"

Hal's face went bright red. He turned away, stepping into the street, staring at the driveway at the top of the cul-de-sac. The farther he walked, the faster Cassidy's heart raced. She tried to motion to Ping to finish up. Somewhere, a clock was ticking. What would happen if Mr. Chase and his mother-in-law stepped out from the bushes? What story would Ping tell Mrs. Yu then?

"Nope," Ping answered. "A real charity case. That's why he's with us." She leaned forward quickly and pecked a kiss on her mother's cheek. "Bye, Mom. See you soon." When Ping turned to the group, Cassidy saw her wipe away tears.

"Be back before dark," Mrs. Yu called out. "Love you!"

"Love you too," said Ping over her shoulder.

She strolled purposefully past Cassidy and Joey into the street. They chased after her, meeting up with Hal, who'd already made it almost halfway through the circle of asphalt.

"You okay?" Joey asked her.

"Fine," Ping said, looking at the ground. "You sure you don't want to stop by your house? Say good-bye to your mom too?"

Joey stumbled backward. "Is that what was happening back there?" Ping didn't answer. "You don't think we're coming back?"

"At the library, we agreed about how far we'd take this," said Ping. "It's a risk, but it's important. Right, Cassidy?"

Cassidy swallowed and nodded slowly.

Joey bit at his lip and tugged at the hem of his T-shirt. "Yeah, but . . . Before, it was all words and promises. Now it's, like, *real*."

Ping sighed. "It isn't going to be easy. But we have to try. We *have* to. The three of us." Everyone stared at Ping as if she'd just spoken in a language none of them had heard before. "Think about it, Hal. You don't need to be here. In the library, you didn't hear the voice. You didn't see the beast. You broke your own curse when you brought back the mannequin. If you want, you can go home."

"And leave you three alone here? After everything we've already been through? You're insane if you think I'm that callous.

And I don't need to say good-bye to my mom. Because I know we're all coming back."

Joey smiled. "Famous last words."

Cassidy felt her stomach clench. She imagined Naomi back in the city, clueless to what was happening out here. What was the last thing they'd said to one another before Cassidy had left for the bus station on Monday? Certainly not *Love you*. Naomi had never been that kind of mother. But then, Cassidy had never been that kind of daughter.

A breeze snagged her hair, pulling it away from her face, as if to show her the path she would take forward. The opening in the trees at the curb howled voicelessly at them. Ursula's driveway was darker now than it had been in the bright light of morning. The afternoon only stretched the shadows thin, giving them an emaciated and starving appearance.

"We'll never be ready," Cassidy said. "So let's just go."

CHAPTER FIFTY-FOUR

THEY MADE THEIR WAY up the driveway more quickly than they had done that morning. Hal and Joey picked up long sharp sticks at the edge of the path and handed one to each of the others, so they'd all have a weapon in case they encountered the house's sentinels. Their dead neighbors.

With every step, Cassidy felt a coldness creeping into her mind. She wasn't sure if it was her body trying to turn off her fear or if the *beast* was already reaching out to her again. She kept seeing movement in the dark woods, doubtful it was all in her head.

One thing she knew for sure: The closer they came to the front steps of the old farmhouse, the louder the humming grew. It had started when they were about halfway up the driveway. Deep. Resonant. Bone rattling. Cassidy was certain it would get louder and louder, maybe so loud it hurt.

The doorway stood open, just as they'd left it earlier. The horrible smell had crept outside. None of them said a word as they climbed the rotting porch stairs. Hal's mannequin lay in the foyer, disguised by the shadows, looking like a dismembered corpse. They paused for a moment before stepping around it, as if the thing that had attacked Hal the night before might rise up with its faceless head and black-taloned hands. Joey asked Cassidy for his flashlight and turned it on. The ghostly light illuminated the dusky space. Dust swirled around them, like tiny insects inspecting their skin for a good spot to settle down and chomp. The stench of the place was overwhelming — a powerful entity in its own right. Cassidy tried to breathe through her mouth, but this didn't stop her from gagging several times as she crossed the room. She squeezed the straps of her backpack and followed Ping through the dark doorway by the base of the stairs. At the end of the hall-way, they found the basement door hanging askew, off its hinges, the padlock lying once more on the floor, smashed bits of the wooden frame scattered around it.

Despite this sight, Cassidy felt comfort as the notebook shifted against her spine, knowing that the pendant was tucked safely inside its pages. The seal of protection. They only had to get to the heart of the house and then throw it inside.

Descending the stairs into the concrete pit, Cassidy wondered how Ping could be so sure this plan would work. Yes, the situation was similar to what happened in Gingerwich, but it wasn't the *same*. Stopping at the bottom of the steps, the group huddled into the corner of the basement. Cassidy listened to Ping's worried, uneven breathing, and she understood that none of them could be certain of anything anymore. Especially not here.

Joey swung the light up so that it lit the other side of the room. In the center of the wall, the black crevice stared back at them, slim like the pupil of a cat's eye. The light rebounded off the floor, illuminating a few feet inside the space. The earth beyond the jag-ged opening looked like it had been carved out or melted away. The garbage and detritus that had filled the hole that morning was now scattered across the floor, having been pushed out by the ani-mated corpses that had been hiding inside.

"Well," said Joey, his voice shaking, "here we are."

"What now?" asked Hal, holding up his stick like a sword.

Ping stepped forward, scraping her own stick along the floor, as if she were trying to let whatever was inside know that they were coming for it.

CHAPTER FIFTY-FIVE

AT THE WALL, Cassidy felt a slight wind blowing past them into the hole, as if a small vacuum was trying to pull them forward. "This is what it wants," she whispered.

"Of course," said Joey. "That's why we're here."

"No. I mean, it's making this really easy for us. Too easy. Just this morning, a bunch of zombies were chasing us. Now, it's as if that never happened."

"In the library," said Ping, "we all heard a voice telling us to *bring it back*. If we are the *it* that the thing wanted, I guess we're following its orders. Maybe it's pleased with us."

"If the beast wants to make this easier for us," said Hal, "it'll only be sorry later." He stepped close to the crevice, waving for Joey to hand over the flashlight.

"Shh," said Cassidy. "Don't let it hear you. Don't even think stuff like that."

"Okay, okay. I'll think about ponies and sunshine. That better?"

Cassidy nodded. "Actually, yes."

A moment of silence settled between them, like a stone dropping into an otherwise still pool of water.

Hal sighed, but managed a smile. "I'm heading in. You guys stay close." Joey handed him the flashlight. Hal turned sideways and squeezed into the opening. Ping went second, followed by Cassidy. Joey brought up the rear, keeping watch over his shoulder in case anything snuck in behind them. He held up his stick, swinging it back and forth like a tail.

The tunnel went on and on, its floor sloping steeply into the earth. Their only light was the one Hal was shining forward. It glistened off slick black rock, catching every now and again on flecks of silica, reflecting like stars in a foreign sky. The earth smelled sour, like low tide and the rot of fallen trees and burning leaves, the tang of it stinging their nostrils the deeper they went.

Cassidy kept her hands on Ping's shoulders, stepping where she stepped so she wouldn't trip and fall. Eventually, the walls of the cave grew wider, the ceiling higher, not by much, but enough so that the air was breathable, and there was space to think.

With every step farther down, Cassidy only wanted to be back at the Tremonts' house, half asleep and tucked under the covers of Tony's big bed, listening to the sounds of her host family getting themselves ready for the day. She wanted to imagine what Rose had planned for her and Joey tomorrow — she'd be happy even if it were digging ditches at the side of the highway. Anything but this.

Every few feet, the tunnel turned slightly to the right, as if spiraling into the earth. Cassidy tried not to imagine how far down they'd traveled or how much farther they'd have to go.

The humming sound had grown. Down in the tunnel, its echoing sounded like a large animal sleeping with a blockage in its throat. Snoring. This might have been soothing if Cassidy wasn't positive that the beast was wide-awake and waiting for them to arrive. This humming was excitement. Pleasure. Like a cat purring.

Hal stopped short. Ping stumbled forward. Cassidy managed to catch herself before the entire group tumbled to the ground. "What's wrong?" Joey whispered from the end of the line.

"This is . . . kinda weird," Hal said, his voice cracking. Peering around one another, the group gazed farther into the tunnel. Hal held the light so it reflected off an object half buried in the dirt several feet ahead. Cassidy squinted and the thing came into focus: a plastic baby-doll head missing its glass eyes.

Hal bent down, and Cassidy whispered harshly for him not to touch it. He made no move to reach for the head; instead he seemed entranced by what he saw deeper in the darkness past the reach of his flashlight. "There's more," he said. "Look." Stepping over the doll head, he swirled the light up to the top of the tunnel, then back down to the floor. Ahead, hundreds of items were shoved into the many small cracks and crevices of earth and stone — water-bloated books, rotting clothes, toys of all sorts, sheets of plastic, hunks of rusted metal, boxes of food, bedding . . . and what looked like several weathered bones, possibly human. They walked on, and the farther they went, the older the items became — broken furniture, wooden picture frames, corroded tools. Almost all of it was coated in thick layers of dust and cobwebs, untouched for what must have been decades. The cavern was becoming what appeared to be some sort of funhouse tunnel, built by a madman. The objects made up the entirety of the walls, ceiling, and floors.

"What is this place?" Ping asked.

"These are its treasures," Cassidy said, feeling her skin shrink close to her muscle. "The ones it's managed to hold on to over years, maybe even before the Chambers house landed on top of it. We're getting closer."

The humming sound vibrated the makeshift walls of the tunnel, rattling glass and metal and plastic.

"What if you just leave the pendant here," said Joey, "with the rest of this stuff?" The light hit his face from below; his eyes looked wide and hollow.

Cassidy stared into the ring of darkness that continued down into the earth. "Because *here* isn't the right spot." She sensed the thing listening to them. "We need to give our gift face-to-face."

Joey shook his head. "I'm not sure that thing even has a face."

They were quiet for a moment. The humming continued, and Cassidy understood that if they stopped here, it would continue for a long time.

"You want to turn around?" Ping asked.

As if to answer her, from the tunnel behind them, they heard a rustling sound descending toward them. The dead had come out of hiding.

Chapter Fifty-Six

"HOLY . . ." JOEY CLOSED his eyes and sighed, his breath ragged, uneven. "This was a terrible idea. The *worst* idea."

"We can't stop now," said Hal. "Not here."

Cassidy raced to follow Ping even as the tunnel of junk began to enclose upon them. The deeper they traveled, the harder it was to step over the debris. Eventually, they ended up crawling on their hands and knees, trying unsuccessfully to avoid whatever looked sharp or jagged. They didn't cry out but kept their pain quiet, as if they might still hide from the things that pursued them.

The humming was now so loud, it was as though it were coming from inside their skulls, like a terrible headache. The vacuum breeze that Cassidy had felt at the tunnel's entrance was stronger down here, practically a wind pulling them forward. Every knocking sound or slithering resonance that echoed from behind pushed Cassidy along. Unwitting tears streaked her face; she ignored them and crawled on. The aroma of death and trash still swirled around them. Once or twice, she had to fight to swallow the bile that was creeping up her esophagus. That voice pulsed in her memory: *Bring it back.* She had no time to be afraid. No choice to turn back.

Rarely did that night when Lou broke down her mother's door haunt her anymore, but now, his voice rang in her head, accompanying the beast's. Everything that she'd recorded in her *Book of Bad Things* formed a segment of a dark tunnel in her mind, a mirror of her current flight. If running from Lou years ago had sent her into a downward spiral from which she'd only just begun to climb out, what would this little excursion do to her? Was this how people ended up insane — experiences like this? Was that how it had happened to Ursula? To her uncle Aidan, before her?

Something snatched at Cassidy's backpack, the straps pulling at her shoulders, and she screamed. Her voice bounded up and down the passage. She twisted her body in the small space, trying to roll away from the thing's clutches until she felt a warm hand on the back of her calf. "Stop," Joey whispered. "You're caught."

She felt him reach past her, toward the roof of the tight tunnel. He released the fabric from what must have been something like a coat hook. Cassidy was free. Her skin burned hot; her lungs felt shrunken by half. "Th-thank you," she said.

"No problem. Be more careful. And quiet."

Grunts and growls sounded at their heels. The dead were catching up.

"Can't you move any faster?" Ping pushed at Hal's rear end.

Hal let out a yelp, then seemed to plunge away, taking the light with him.

CHAPTER FIFTY-SEVEN

"HAL!" PING CRIED OUT. Then, suddenly, she too dropped with a gasp into a void.

Cassidy froze. She could make out a ledge several feet ahead of her, past which a vast nothingness rippled like a dark pool. "What happened?" Joey whispered, frantic. "Where'd they go?"

"I dunno. I dunno. What do we do?" Were her friends hurt? Or worse? And was this her fault? She wanted to close her eyes and disappear. A simple wish. Down here, with the suctioning breeze and the voices and the vibrating air, it almost seemed possible. A dim glow illuminated the dark space beyond the ledge, and Cassidy brought herself back into her body. "Hello?" she whispered. "Is that you, Hal? Ping?"

What if it wasn't them, but something else that knew how to glow in the darkness? She listened to Joey's breath behind her. She hoped he still held onto the stick he'd taken from the driveway; she'd lost her own without even realizing it.

She eased toward the light and peeked over the edge. To her relief, she saw Hal and Ping lying at the bottom of a steep slope of even more garbage. They both whimpered in pain.

Ping sat up slowly, glancing up from where she'd fallen. She grabbed the flashlight that Hal had let go of during his tumble and shined it into Cassidy's eyes. Cassidy waved for her to shine the light away, then slowly climbed down into what appeared to be an enormous room, a spherical cave, the edges of which were almost too far to properly discern. "Come on, Joey," she said. "They're okay."

She began to make her way down the slope, stepping on stuffed animals, a surfboard, an antique writing desk. And bones. More bones. She tried not to think about that as she slid the last few feet to where Hal and Ping had landed. Seconds later, Joey crawled toward them from out of a blanket of darkness.

"Everyone all right?" Hal asked. The group huddled together in a makeshift nest of cardboard boxes, chips of wood, and the remains of some sort of flag.

Ping swung the light around, trying to get a sense of where they were. But the light wasn't powerful enough to reach the ceiling of this new space. And in front of them was only more junk.

"What now?" Joey asked. "Is this it? The center of the vortex?"

"Looks like it might be," said Ping. "But where is the . . . the *beast*?"

"It's quiet," said Cassidy, glancing around blindly.

"Too quiet," said Ping.

"The humming stopped."

Joey stood, shoving the point of his stick into the rubble at his feet. "Maybe it's gone?"

The four listened to the new silence for a moment — only for a moment, because seconds later, the silence was broken by a rustling sound that came from all around them.

Ping swung the flashlight ahead to find that the piles of garbage were shifting. Or rather, Cassidy understood, something *underneath* the garbage was moving.

CHAPTER FIFTY-EIGHT

"GET BACK!" Cassidy shouted. "Toward the tunnel!"

Ping illuminated the path up the slope from which they'd come. But the dark patch where they'd emerged was filled with a round, pale face. Owen Chase reached out toward them with two filthy, fat arms, blocking the way. Cassidy didn't need to see the others behind him to know that they were there. They hadn't been chasing them in order to catch them. The dead had been pushing the group forward and had now sealed the tunnel shut. The exit was filled with their bodies, their grasping nails, their gnashing teeth.

Hal screamed. Everyone turned to him. Ping's flashlight showed the loose papers and fabrics near their feet were being dispersed by the large thing that traveled just below the surface of debris. It moved through the garbage in a long line, coiling, swirling, spiraling, and roiling the mess all around them. The group backed into one another, forming a trembling column of flesh in the middle of the sea of waste.

As Cassidy watched the movement at the cavern's floor, she noticed a length of the creature breach the surface, its body pitch-black and armored with luminescent scales like a giant snake. She remembered what she'd seen at the college library, the thing moving through the next aisle. The beast had sent a vision of itself to her when she'd been alone in the rows of bookshelves, when it had instructed her to *Bring it back!*

It. It. She was *it*. The beast imagined her as a mere object, something to own, to keep.

Its resonant voice filled the darkness now. This time, however, it shouted harshly, again and again: *Mine! Mine!!! MINE!!!*

Cassidy couldn't breathe, couldn't move. She waited, paralyzed for the beast to fully emerge from below, wrapping its coils around all of them, squeezing. It wanted their lives, or at least their corpses. They were stupid to have come here expecting a chance to survive, to beat this thing. They would die in this fetid pit, and no one would ever know. Not Janet or Benji. Not Rose or Dennis or Deb or Tony. Not Levi Stanton. Not even her mother, Naomi, who might finally care what had happened to her only daughter, if only for curiosity's sake. None of them would learn the truth.

Vaguely, she thought she heard someone calling her name, and only when Joey elbowed her in the ribs did she understand that he was trying to help her remove her backpack.

Of course! The pendant! *The seal of protection.* She'd forgotten the reason they'd come. Was it possible that the beast had stolen the thought?

She slipped her arms out of the straps. Joey held up the backpack. Cassidy undid the zipper and reached inside, feeling around for her book at the bottom. She pulled it out, opened to the page where the small package had been folded. The plastic baggie fell into her hand. Inside, the pentacle glistened in the ghostly glow of the flashlight. She tucked the notebook under her arm.

Her heart shuddered.

The object, wrapped up in plastic, looked so ordinary against her skin. This tiny thing was going to save them, the town, the world?

CHAPTER FIFTY-NINE

"I don't know what to do," Cassidy said.

"I guess we should tell the beast what it means," said Ping, glancing briefly at the ever-shifting floor. "Then offer it up."

Tell the beast? How would that work? *Umm, Mr. Beast. I have something to tell you. . . .* Cassidy blinked, shook the ridiculous image away. Okay, Ping may be right, but would the beast listen?

MINE!!! Its voice rippled against her brain, filling the cavern . . . or her head, she couldn't tell which.

Her hands trembling, Cassidy ripped open the baggie. The tiny links shivered as she lifted the chain from her palm. The star swung from it like a pendulum. Back and forth. Hypnotically. She tore her gaze away and turned toward the ocean of darkness and garbage.

Mine!!!

"Y-yes," she muttered, trying to find her voice again. She spoke to the air, unsure where to focus. "This is for you." She held up the chain with one hand.

"Say what it means," Ping whispered. "What it represents."

"Th-the star is an . . . ancient symbol of protection," Cassidy said, remembering Ping's own words and the passage from the library book. "This pendant will seal up this space and stop your . . . curse. It is our gift to you."

The humming began again, that pleasure sound. Its tiny, pervasive vibration filled her body, every cell. Cassidy gagged.

Miiiiine, the voice whispered, as if finally satisfied.

Clutching the star pendant in her left hand, Cassidy swung the necklace back over her shoulder, then whipped it forward.

Ping followed it with the flashlight beam as it landed several dozen feet away, disappearing into the piles of trash. The thing beneath the garbage thrashed and swiveled, struggling to find the new gift amongst all of its others. After a few seconds it seemed to settle down next to it, pulling its coils in close, as if quieted after a meal. *Mine,* it whispered again.

Cassidy waited for something profound to happen. A clap of thunder. A flash of light. An earthquake. A booming voice. But nothing came.

In fact the room was as still as they'd first found it.

"I think it worked," said Joey.

"Let's get out of here," Hal said, stepping away from where Cassidy had tossed the star.

But back up the slope, Owen Chase howled at them from the tunnel entry, reaching toward them with his shattered fingernails and bruised skin.

"If the curse is broken," Ping whispered, "then why is Mr. Chase still awake?"

Owen clutched at the sides of the tunnel, finally pulling himself forward. He tumbled onto the slope, spilling end-over-end toward them. His mother-in-law, Millie, appeared behind him. She too began to struggle out from the tight space.

"That's the thing," Cassidy said, her voice flat, her eyes wide. "I don't think the curse is broken."

Owen skidded to a stop several feet away, lifting his large round head, staring at them with milky eyes. He opened his lips in an oozing snarl.

"What do you mean?" Joey said, his voice rising, lifting the point of the stick to keep Mr. Chase at bay. The dead man swiped at Joey, lunging toward him. Joey whacked its shoulder. "You gave it that *seal* thing."

"Yeah, I did," Cassidy answered, distracted, scrambling away from Owen's reach. "I guess it didn't work."

CHAPTER SIXTY

AN AVALANCHE OF TRASH spilled down the slope as Millie tumbled to the bottom. When she settled to a stop, she struggled to stand, to advance on the group. More sounds came from above. Ursula and Aidan were emerging from the tunnel as well. Soon, they too would be crawling down the incline.

Cassidy paid them little mind. She stumbled backward, twisting her ankle on something under her feet. When she'd righted herself, the group followed her, easing quickly away from the dead people.

The plan had failed. Their seal of protection was not going to protect them after all. Cassidy burned. How stupid could they be? The strategy had been flimsy, culled together from bits and pieces of magazine articles and a single article of academic folklore. Why had they thought that some random piece of jewelry would be powerful enough to kill an ageless evil beast, or to destroy what might be a portal to another world, another dimension where things such as ageless evil beasts existed?

Maybe if the pendant had belonged to them. Maybe if it had once protected any of them from danger. But that was the thing about objects — and people, for that matter — it takes time and effort to forge a relationship, to create experiences that become memories, for those memories to sink in, become lessons. To understand the lessons and use them to make choices. It was the choice that saves you. Or destroys you. Of course the pendant wouldn't work. Their present had only been a piece of junk.

The four dead bodies rose from the makeshift floor, focusing their milky gazes on the four young, living people who cowered away from them.

Even though the beast was distracted, shifting in the garbage behind them seemingly entranced by its gift, Cassidy cringed, not wanting to be so close to it. But she stood her ground. So the pendant wouldn't neutralize the vortex, but it might buy them some time. "When I say go," Cassidy whispered to the group, "we run. As fast as we can back up the slope. We're faster than these freaks."

"Unless the dog is waiting for us," said Hal, gazing past the dead toward the dark opening above them. "Up there."

"And what about the rest of it?" Joey asked. "We'll never be able to leave this place. The beast is still alive. The vortex, or whatever this place is, remains the same and so does the curse."

"Joey's right," Ping nodded. She wiped at her eyes. "We can't leave. It's our . . . our duty to stay."

Cassidy turned to find Ursula's corpse staring at her. The dead woman moved her mouth, making wet, smacking sounds as if she were trying to speak. Cassidy figured she was merely chewing on her tongue. There were no words left in the thing's empty head. The woman's lifeless eyes, sunken in her skull, were so different from the shimmering orbs that Cassidy had encountered in her dream and at the library. Ursula's ghost — her soul, what was left of the real Ursula Chambers — had led her here. *Come in*, she'd said. Why would the spirit have singled out Cassidy, to invite her inside the house when she'd demanded that so many others stay away?

A seal of protection. To stop the beast, close the vortex.

The star pendant had meant nothing to Cassidy, but she'd been carrying something else that did. An object that, for the past few years, she'd had with her at all times, rarely letting it out of her sight, an object that she'd often placed under her pillow to protect her from panic, from anxiety, from nightmares.

The four dead folk stepped forward, swinging out their arms wildly, forcing the group backward, toward the hidden coils of the beast.

A *true* seal of protection. Cassidy had it tucked under her arm, pressed against her ribcage, next to her heart. *The Book of Bad Things*.

Chapter Sixty-One

"Joey, Hal, don't take your eyes off these guys," Cassidy said, stepping away from her dead neighbors and toward the place where the beast had shifted down into the debris. "Ping, hold up the flashlight for me. I have an idea."

The others listened, trusting her, even if they didn't understand. Joey swatted at the air between himself and the dead with his stick. Beside him, Hal dug up a wooden table leg from the junk heap. He jabbed it at the skinny brown thing that had once been Aidan Chambers. The corpse grabbed at the leg with such ferocity, Hal yelped, nearly falling backward. He jabbed at Aidan again, this time pounding him directly in the chest. Old bones snapped, echoing like felled branches breaking during a hike through the woods.

Cassidy led Ping several feet away to a safer distance. "What are you doing?" Ping whispered, reluctant, panicked. Cassidy took the notebook from under her arm and opened to the first page. "Hold up the light," she whispered. "Please."

Ping glanced at the book, an understanding sparking in her eyes. Quickly, she pointed the flashlight, keeping her hand steady, the beam making the bone-white pages glow like a flare. Cassidy began to read the words she'd written, her voice steady, strong. "Cassidy's Book of Bad Things, Entry Number One: Intruders."

The flashlight flickered. The air in the cavern pulsed. Cassidy felt a pressure in her skull, and her vision was squeezed into a point. "I was home alone, tossing and turning on the couch, when I heard someone at the door." The world was tiny and Cassidy was enormous, like Alice in Wonderland, drinking the tonic, eating the cakes. The beast had invaded her head. It did not like what she was doing. Cassidy clung to the thought that she must continue, no matter what it tried to make her see or hear or feel. She shook away the disconcerting sensation of shrinking, of growing, of her skin squeezing at her like sausage casing, instead focusing on her words, finding her voice again, calling out, louder this time. "He rattled the knob, testing to see if it was unlocked. And I knew right then that I was in trouble."

The beast called back — *NO! NO! NO!* — its hum and growl nearly drowning out Cassidy's recitation. But she kept her eyes on the page, feeling a tiny bit of comfort that Ping stood beside her. Behind her, the boys were shouting at the dead to stay away. She kept on reading the first entry, her words telling the tale of Lou and Naomi, and meeting Mr. Stanton. The story didn't feel like a story as it escaped her lips, but instead like a prayer.

The bowl-like floor of the cavern trembled, the garbage shifting like sand. A coil of wide black spine erupted out from the debris several steps ahead of her. Cassidy gasped for breath, squashing the impulse to shout out, to turn and run. The thing was rising, filled with shuddering rage, whipping its body through the space, flinging its treasures every which way. A brown leather boot flew toward the girls, smashing Ping's shoulder. The flashlight flew from her grasp, landing with a crunch a few feet from where Joey was tussling with Mrs. Moriarty. Both girls whirled toward the lost light.

Ping and Joey both went for the flashlight. He grabbed it first, holding it up to Ping, not noticing that Mrs. Moriarty had dragged herself to within biting distance of his ankle. Ping leapt over Joey and landed on the dead woman, grinding her knees into the corpse's back. "Go!" she shouted at him. "I've got this."

Scrambling to his feet, Joey grunted and then shouted out to

Cassidy, "Keep reading!" He panted as he sidled up beside her, taking Ping's place, shining the light at the notebook.

Cassidy refused to lose focus. She turned the page and started on the second entry.

STOP! STOP NOW!

Since Joey's flashlight was directed at the notebook, the group could not see very far outside of its reach. Still, from her peripheral vision, Cassidy knew that the black snake-thing had fully risen from its hiding place. It had no beginning and no end, no head, no tail, but instead was an endless loop of iridescently dark flesh. Its body was pulled in on itself like a spring, ready to explode outward to careen into all of them with the force of a racing train. Cassidy read faster, faster. She turned another page, began the next entry.

Then, something strange happened — something even stranger than everything that had already happened. The coils of snake, roiling with fury, slowly rose out of the crater, fully hovering in the space above the garbage. Its mass was the size of a whale. Cassidy didn't allow herself to look at it directly.

NOOO!! its voice called out, echoing with an unbelieving fury that, somehow, by some strange magic, it had been separated from its beloved cache of trash and treasure. A few bits of junk rose up with the beast, as if the thing were trying to pull close whatever it could.

"Keep reading!" Joey shouted.

Cassidy blinked and found the page again. She shouted her words over the thing's raucous din, the shaking of the pit, the objects lifting and falling to the ground, smashing and crashing, breaking against one another.

The beast ascended, its body compressing, its coils tightening so that it took the shape of a small planet. A moon. An orb. Soon, the thing seemed unable to move at all but only screamed word-lessly at the girl who had come to destroy it.

Cassidy could feel its pain, its rage, its terror. She felt exhausted, the words blurring on the page, but she read on.

Around the black beast, a blue fire appeared. Quickly, the orb was engulfed. The beast's skin puckered, searing in the flame. It seemed to shrink, pressing into a smaller shape as if by a garbage truck's trash compactor. Or a black hole. Panicked, the dying thing released a new sound, a new voice, different from its approximation of human language. Something that Cassidy would not have been able to describe if someone were to ask later. All she knew was that the beast was speaking its own language, a counter spell. The flame began to diminish, and the beast emitted a wail, a growl, a belch, a shriek, all combining into a deafening din that Cassidy understood to be a hoot of triumph.

The orb began to grow again.

CHAPTER SIXTY-TWO

PING AND HAL HOWLED, and Cassidy and Joey turned to find that the dead neighbors, though bloodied and battered, had managed to advance on the two, knocking them to the ground, disarming them. Joey's sharp stick and Hal's table leg lay nearby. Owen Chase scrambled toward Ping, his mouth open, leaking a dark liquid. Old Aidan had fallen farther back, seemingly unable to move. But Millie Moriarty and Ursula walked, hunched over, in the direction of Hal, reaching for him like a pair of hungry elderly friends out to lunch at a Chinese buffet.

Joey shoved the flashlight into Cassidy's hand, then dashed toward the fray. Cassidy started to follow, but Joey called over his shoulder, "Stay! Finish this!"

The blue light behind her illuminated much of the dark space now. Cassidy watched Joey kick Owen Chase to the ground, stomping on his grasping fingers. He handed Ping the stick, helped her stand, and together they beat back Millie and Ursula.

But as the beast continued to whisper its ancient words, its own eldritch prayer, the blue light began to fade. Cassidy turned back to the black orb, the blue flame now a thin coat of color, quickly dimming. The work she had done, the reading, her words, was being neutralized by the beast. She stepped closer, struggling to shine the flashlight on her page. She called out more of what she'd written, the collection of memories and beliefs. Words poured from her mouth, making her throat raw. Her energy fed the fire like oxygen and it began to consume the monster once more. But the beast countered, yowling its own selfish thoughts, radiating its pitiful sensations of loneliness, obsession, anger.

How was one girl, not yet thirteen years old, supposed to defeat something of such incredible power?

For a moment, Cassidy felt as though she almost understood why the beast needed what it needed, why it did what it had done, what it continued to do. She had experienced similar wild desires. But she'd controlled the desires, channeled the thoughts into the words she'd written in the book. She clutched the cardboard cover, which had grown slick and damp with her sweat.

She felt the beast rummaging around in her head, picking through her memories, searching for weakness, for fear. What it didn't seem to understand was that the notebook and her pen had protected her from the darkness that lived inside her. For this reason, the book had always been the most important thing. Or had it?

Cassidy briefly wondered if she'd treated the book like the beast had treated its hoard.

Bring it back to me. . . .

"I have to let it go," Cassidy whispered to herself.

She stepped forward. The black orb was almost directly over her now. The blue flame was like ice. Its freezing energy billowed out, blowing her hair back from her forehead. She shivered as cold penetrated her core. The beast's voice was an anguished cry now, begging her to stay away. Cassidy tucked the flashlight under her arm. Staring up into the blinding blue, she gripped her notebook between her fingers. Her seal of protection.

"Here," Cassidy called out. "Another present. You're gonna love it." For a moment, the beast quieted, then, as if understanding what kind of gift this small girl was presenting, it screeched, the noise of it nearly knocking Cassidy off her feet. She dug her sneakers into the shifting pit, steadied her arm, then drew the book back behind her head. Ripping her hand forward, she felt the object slip from her fingers, and for a moment, she wondered if she'd made a mistake, letting go of the thing that had kept her safe for so long. But as it careened across the short distance and connected with the blue blaze and the dark entity trapped within, Cassidy felt a sudden freedom. A lightness.

Peace.

The flames flashed white. Cassidy was lifted into the air and thrown backward. She landed on her spine, on something sharp; a burst of pain briefly detonated in her tailbone. She barely registered the feeling.

From her spot in the hollow, she had the perfect view for what came next.

The black orb telescoped inward, the blue flame grew outward, and with a small pop and a sigh, the space over the pit of garbage went blank. The air grew still, and other than the ringing in her ears, the world was uncannily, eerily silent.

CHAPTER SIXTY-THREE

THIS PEACE LASTED ONLY a moment. The sound that Cassidy had expected earlier, when she'd tossed the star-shaped pendant at the beast, finally came. A great cracking sound rang out, as though the unseen stone over their heads had split, and the ground shook.

The flashlight now lay several feet from Cassidy. The blur of the explosion hung in the center of her vision, but she managed to reach out for the light. Joey and Hal and Ping struggled to stand. The dead lay all around them, finally unmoving, lifeless. Cassidy rolled over onto her hands and knees, and as another quake shook the cavern, she called out, "You guys okay?"

"I think so," said Joey. He waved his weapon — the stick he'd snatched up from the driveway — at the corpses at his feet. "They all just dropped."

"Yeah, right when you threw the book at the creature," said Ping. "You broke the curse, Cassidy!"

Another trembling rattled the cave. Far off, something large crashed to the floor, causing the debris beneath their feet to move.

"How about we congratulate one another later," said Hal, "*after* we get the heck out of this place?"

Cassidy ran to the group, throwing her arms wide, encompassing all of them. She didn't care what Hal thought. They had to celebrate this moment, if only for a moment. To her surprise, each of them hugged her back. Together they stood, a circle of warmth in this place of chill darkness.

She glanced down at the faces of her fallen neighbors, who now looked even paler than before. Ursula lay in her velvet burgundy funeral gown, her eyes finally closed. "We can't just leave them here."

"We can't carry them," Hal said.

Another rumble. Another crash.

"He's right," Ping said. "We've got to get out of here."

"But how do we get back out?" Joey asked, glancing up the slope toward the spot where they'd come in. The trash had shifted, covering up the tunnel entrance.

"It's up there somewhere," said Cassidy.

The group moved purposefully up the hill, but slid several feet down when tremors rocked the room and trash loosened beneath them. The quakes were coming more and more frequently. If the vortex had created this space, now that it was shuttered, the ceiling might not hold much longer. Around the spot where they thought they'd entered, they tossed away the garbage — bags, clothes, buckets of dried paint, board games, a smashed television set. But every time they picked up an object to move it out of the way, something else moved into its place.

A colossal crash shook the ground at the bottom of the hill. Cassidy swung the flashlight to find a massive chunk of earth had dropped, and a cloud of dust and dirt was swirling their way. "What are we going to do?" she asked, having lost all the power that her voice had contained only minutes earlier.

No one answered.

And then, of course, the flashlight blinked out.

CHAPTER SIXTY-FOUR

PING SQUEALED, CLUTCHING AT Cassidy's hand. Cassidy squeezed back.

"Stupid battery!" Joey said in the pitch darkness.

"We're dead," Hal added.

"No," said Cassidy. "We're not. We stay calm. We do what we need to do." The night that Lou had broken into her apartment flashed into her mind. She'd never thought she would make it away from him. And afterward, she'd never thought she'd escape her fear. But she did survive. And she did escape. It had taken effort, but then again, the truly important things always did. "Get down. Dig. Dig!"

The group worked. Sounds of debris being tossed echoed all around. Long seconds passed. Another distant crash. Dirt rained down. Cassidy braced herself, immediately feeling ridiculous, as if tightening her muscles would protect her from a three-ton boulder dropping from above.

"Did someone say something?" Joey asked, a disembodied voice in the dark.

"I heard someone whisper," Ping said from somewhere nearby.

"What was it?" Hal asked.

But Joey didn't have time to answer. Another voice came from somewhere beneath the layer of debris. *Here*, it whispered. This was followed by a dog's muffled bark.

Blind, Cassidy leaned toward the spot where the sounds had come.

"Is it another trap?" This was Ping.

"No," Cassidy said, reaching into the pile of junk, pulling it away, feeling for the ledge and the passage from which they'd earlier tumbled. "It's Ursula. And Lucky. They're trying to help."

They crawled then stood and stumbled through the blackened, garbage-strewn tunnel, talking constantly to one another — *Here, Here, Here, Here* — so they wouldn't become separated. Cassidy reached out every few feet, feeling for Ping's shoulder. Behind her, she felt Joey do the same. They moved quickly, the ground trembling, great pounding sounds of collapsing rock echoing up the passage from behind them. Once they reached the section of the path that was free from the beast's "collection," they began to run, feeling for the walls that narrowed with every step, every turn.

Continuing the ascent blindly, Cassidy wondered if this might all be a dream, for certainly it had all the hallmarks. Maybe, in a moment or two, she'd wake up in Tony's bed, or for that matter, on the small couch in her mother's apartment, her heart racing, sweat on her brow. But she wasn't dreaming, she soon discovered. A dim light appeared up ahead. They all cried out, in relief, in pain, in shock, as they tumbled from the crevice onto the trash-strewn floor of the Chambers house basement.

Moments later, the steady rumbling sound grew louder, the earth shaking as the passage crumbled behind the wall. A torrent of dust and dirt belched forth from the crack in the concrete, coating their already grimy bodies.

The group scrambled backward toward the stairs. As Cassidy raced up the shadowy steps toward the broken doorway, she sighed, glancing over her shoulder at the last of the debris littering the floor. The stray clothes. Kitchen utensils. Worn-out basketball sneakers. All useless pieces of garbage and yet, the cause of so much trouble.

Outside, the group didn't stop, limping along until they'd reached the asphalt of the cul-de-sac.

The sun was shining. Pristine, puffy clouds were scattered across a perfect blue sky. The air was hot, but a breeze blew through the trees behind them. They'd made it out. The curse was broken. The ordeal was over. This was the end.

But as Cassidy stood in awkward silence huddled with her friends, old and new, she couldn't help but believe that this was also a moment of beginning. And she wasn't sure if it was going to be a good thing or a bad thing.

Now she had no book in which to write, no blank pages to help her figure it out.

She glanced back up the shadowed driveway path, tree branches dancing casually in the breeze, as if everything were normal, as if monsters did not exist, as if friendships didn't end, as if summers lasted forever, and she imagined her pages buried somewhere deep underground, along with the bodies and everything else the beast had stolen.

─{THREE MONTHS LATER}─
CASSIDY & THE FAMILY

IT WAS OCTOBER IN BROOKLYN, New York.

Most of the trees surrounding the Long Meadow in Prospect Park had begun to turn, the leaves transforming the green landscape of the Indian summer into a festive costume. Specks of red and yellow and orange flickered across the grass, blowing without care toward the whispering arc of traffic rushing through Grand Army Plaza.

In the southeast quadrant of the giant traffic oval stood the central branch of the Brooklyn Public Library, the golden bas-relief sculptures that surrounded its main entrance glittering in the afternoon sunlight like gods on earth.

Cassidy Bean sat on the wide front steps, tapping her toes against the cold stone beneath her. She watched the pedestrians scurrying about, imagining that from high up, they'd all look as insignificant as a bunch of insects. Since the end of summer, Cassidy had felt the same. Small. So, so small.

"You see 'em?" Her friend Janet sat down beside her. Janet's twin, Benji, continued to swing upside down on the stainless steel railing that ran alongside the stairway, lost in his own head.

"Not yet," Cassidy answered. "Maybe I should have told them I'd meet them at the subway entrance across the plaza."

"Give 'em some credit," said Janet, smiling. "Not every tourist is completely helpless."

"The Tremonts aren't tourists," Cassidy said, bumping Janet's shoulder playfully. "They're my friends."

"Well, I hope they get here soon," said Janet. "Mr. Stanton's reading —"

"It doesn't start for an hour," Cassidy interrupted. "We're fine."

"I can't wait to see him," Benji chirped. "I've read all his books."

"You have not," Janet said, irritated.

Benji dropped his arms from the railing, dangling his upper body from the bar like a monkey. "Well, I read one of them."

"He read a *page* of one of them," Janet whispered. The girls giggled as Benji sidled up next to them.

"Are you laughing at me?" he asked, curious.

"Yup," Cassidy said simply, which made all three of them laugh even harder. It felt good. She had only just recently begun to feel like herself again. Starting school had certainly helped.

In the couple of long weeks between the end of her time in Whitechapel and the beginning of the semester, Cassidy wondered if she might be slipping back to her old ways. She'd had moments of anxiety. Panic. Feeling lost in places she knew well and desperate at night whenever Naomi continued to lock herself in her bedroom. It wasn't only her apartment that was weird. Before her return from Whitechapel, she would never have expected the entire city to feel as overwhelming as it now did. The eardrum-breaking noise of the train through the stations. The crowds of people stampeding obliviously against the lights into crosswalks. The flashing advertisements on top of speeding cabs. Even the store windows packed with everything anyone might ever need seemed like too much.

Everywhere she looked, she saw *stuff,* and the *stuff* always reminded her of what she'd seen in the cavern beneath Ursula Chambers's house. The junk. The garbage. The filth. And the nameless creature whose desires had created the pit, had destroyed lives, had almost taken hers.

The rest of the summer had floated past her, past Joey and Ping, like a fantasy. Cassidy and Joey finished out the art program at the college, ending up with a small portfolio they were allowed to take home. Rose filled the rest of their days with scrumptious meals, with trips to the library, with movies and games and road trips beyond the Delaware Water Gap, which Cassidy was so thankful for.

Tales of Ursula's ghost evaporated from the town almost immediately after that horrible Friday. Cassidy took comfort in the idea that the woman had finally found rest after a life lived in constant fear. At night, before bed, Cassidy prayed for her, grateful for her sacrifice, feeling saddened that no one would ever know what the old woman had done to keep the town safe.

In the evenings, she and Joey had met up with Ping and sometimes Hal, sitting on one of their front porches or back patios, a citronella candle burning nearby to keep away the bugs. They'd talk about what they could remember, about what they'd thought happened, about whether or not it had *actually* happened. They'd agreed to keep their story to themselves. How would they even begin to explain to anyone who hadn't been there, hadn't seen what they'd seen, when they themselves weren't even sure?

Still, there'd been bits of proof scattered around the neighborhood from the day of the final confrontation. Hal's parents came home from work to discover what was left of poor Lucky's body lying in their foyer. Hal had felt horrible claiming ignorance, especially when the local police couldn't provide answers either. However, he'd delivered the remains to the empty grave in Joey's backyard himself, helping Joey dig another hole, then saying a final farewell to the unfortunate animal.

About a week after that, a land surveyor discovered unstable ground around Ursula's old house. A wide fissure had opened up by its foundation, reaching out several feet, a darkness eating at the earth. His team determined that a sinkhole had formed in the area. The house was in imminent danger of collapse and was condemned. The residents of Chase Estates of course had raised a fuss, wondering if their own homes were safe. But after more investigation, Whitechapel was satisfied that the only rotten ground was far beyond the end of the cul-de-sac, up on the hill.

The farmhouse would be torn down. Someday. But Cassidy's time in Whitechapel would end before that happened.

No one ever found the missing bodies. It was a mystery that would haunt the area for years to come. Their story would eventually capture the attention of the editors of Ping's favorite magazine. And when Whitechapel eventually appeared on the cover of *Strange State*, Ping would ask her mother to buy her three copies — one for reading, one that she was certain would be destroyed by her brothers, and one for safekeeping. Someday, maybe, somehow, the truth would come out. But for now, Cassidy believed that even Ursula would conclude that the story of the ley lines, of the vortex, of the nameless beast was best tucked away on a secret shelf in their memories.

Across the street, a tall, thin woman waved. Cassidy stood, squinting through the slanting sunlight. When she noticed the others standing beside the woman, Cassidy jumped up and down. Ping and Joey held hands, mirroring her own excitement with their own little leaps. Dennis smiled and led the group through the crosswalk and up the steps to Cassidy, throwing his arms around her.

Janet and Benji backed away as the rest of the group joined in, enveloping her in corduroy and fleece and wool.

Rose stepped back and glanced up, taking in the grand sight of the library. "This is so beautiful! What a wonderful place to find you."

Cassidy blushed, glancing between Ping and Joey. "I thought you'd like it. The train ride was okay?"

She introduced the Tremonts and Ping to her friends. When Benji shook Ping's hand, he went uncharacteristically quiet, and Janet threw Cassidy a smirk. She had to keep herself from bursting out giggling again.

They spent the next half hour sitting on the wide steps. Rose and Dennis filled Cassidy in on what was going on with Deb and Tony and their "boring" lives in Whitechapel. Cassidy filled them in on her life in Brooklyn. Then, she led them into the library, to the auditorium, where her neighbor, Levi Stanton, was leading a panel discussion about crime novelists.

It turned out, Dennis had long been a huge fan. After the event, he treated the author and everyone else to dinner at a soul-food restaurant around the corner, where they became entangled in an intricate discussion about other authors of the genre.

Nestled at the far end of the long table, the kids were lost in their own world. Before the food arrived, Joey reached into a shopping bag and removed a small rectangular parcel, wrapped neatly in plain brown paper. He handed it to Cassidy.

"What's this?"

"A replacement." Joey smiled. "It's from all of us." He glanced at Ping who blushed. "Hal chipped in too."

He didn't need to say more for Cassidy to understand what was inside. She slowly removed the wrapping, revealing a leather cover and several hundred blank pages. For a moment, she was overcome. The room tilted. Her breath shrunk. Another *Book of Bad Things*? She wasn't sure if she was ready to return to the dark places, to look closer into the shadows, or if she ever would be ready. "Thank you so much," she whispered. She turned the book end-over-end, examining every nook, crease, stitch.

The object was beautiful in a way that something new can never be. They must have found it at Junkland. She squeezed the book between her fingers, understanding that she didn't have to go back again, not if she didn't want to. "I know exactly what I'm going to write in it when I get home."

"Oh yeah?" said Joey. "What's that?"

Cassidy glanced at the group huddled around the table. Her host parents chatted with her favorite neighbor a few chairs away. Her friends, Janet and Benji, smiled at her. And Ping and Joey simply sighed, contented to be together again. She couldn't imagine a more perfect moment. Her heart hurt that it wouldn't last. Still, she smiled. "I'm going to write about today."

ACKNOWLEDGMENTS

FIRST, I NEED TO THANK the whole team at Scholastic Press for the unbelievably attentive work they do, especially my editor and friend Nick Eliopulos, who is a champion of all things odd and offbeat. How many times can I say I would not be writing these books if it weren't for him? I'm sure I'll say it again — many, many times.

A huge thank you must go to my agent Barry Goldblatt, whose pep talks and enthusiasm keep me sane through crazy times. And thank you to Tricia Ready for all that she does.

A big hug to my friends and family. I am very lucky to have all of you in my life. I want to send out particular gratitude to my cousins Madison and Gabby. They asked me to put them in this book, and I don't think they'll have to look very hard to find themselves in the main characters.

Most of all, I must mention one of the best humans I know. Daniel Villela makes me realize everyday that my life is a *Good Thing*, and for that, I am eternally grateful.

ABOUT THE
AUTHOR

DAN POBLOCKI is the author of *The Stone Child*, *The Nightmarys*, and the Mysterious Four series. His recent books, *The Ghost of Graylock* and *The Haunting of Gabriel Ashe*, were Junior Library Guild selections and made the American Library Association's Best Fiction for Young Adults list in 2013 and 2014. Dan lives in Brooklyn with two scaredy-cats and a growing collection of very creepy toys. Visit him at www.danpoblocki.com.

❖